Murder on Hogtown Creek

A North Florida Mystery

M. D. Abrams

BookLocker.com, Inc.
2009

For Dorie

Also by M.D. Abrams

Murder at Wakulla Springs: A North Florida Mystery
(Winner of the Florida Book Award for Popular Fiction)

Murder on the Prairie: A North Florida Mystery

Murder on Hogtown Creek

A North Florida Mystery

Acknowledgments

Author Frank Robinson told me, "You have to write at least one more book and make it a trilogy." This is the third book in my North Florida Mystery series. I am indebted to friend and neighbor, Shirley Lasseter, for my choice of Hogtown Creek as the initial setting for the story. She led me hiking through a section of the creek, very near my house, which I had failed to explore during the 20 years I lived here. It is beautiful and I now treasure the area. It is there the murder is discovered.

It has been my intention, in all three North Florida mysteries, to feature ecological and historic sites of significance in this part of the state, as well as the environmental issues surrounding them. Hogtown Creek may be just a *tumbling stream*, as one writer noted, but it holds great value to residents of Gainesville—humans and other creatures.

Thanks are due for the excellent information about the creek, which I received from Alachua County Environmental Protection Department members, Director Chris Bird and Robin Hallbourg. Jim Myles created the simplified and readable map of the creek. My research on historic information about Hogtown Creek, was facilitated by the Curator of the P.K. Yonge Library of Florida History, James Cusiak, and staff in the Smathers Libraries at the University of Florida. Thanks also to a chance meeting with Stephen Carr, in which he told me where I might find out about the hogs in Hogtown Creek.

As a member of Florida Defenders of the Environment (FDE), and one-time project director, I had a wealth of information about the Ocklawaha River and Rodman/Kirkpatrick Dam. I am greatly indebted, however, to several people who informed my understanding of current issues and feelings about river restoration.

Karen Ahlers, President of the Putnam County Environmental Council, Inc, provided me with insights about the fight to restore and protect the St. Johns and Ocklawaha rivers. She also introduced me to Captain Erika Ritter whose family has long lived alongside the river. Captain Ritter and Karen took me on a wonderful boat ride to see the Eureka Lock and Dam, and to witness the restoration of the

Ocklawaha's forested banks which had been clear cut by Barge Canal work. The scene debunked the myth that it would take 100 years before the forest and wildlife would return. FDE board member Kristina Jackson and Executive Director, Nick Williams, were helpful in providing information about the Ocklawaha restoration. I am also grateful to Major Gary Bowling, Putnam County Sheriff's Office, for being a resource about the criminal aspects of the story.

A section of the book deals with the issue of homelessness. I believe it to be a human tragedy and a moral failing in our country. Arupa Freeman, an "angel" to the homeless, took me out on her Home Van, which provides them and their pets with food and other essentials. She also walked me through tent city, now outlawed, and introduced me to residents. Jon DeCarmine is dedicated to solving related issues, as Executive Director of the Alachua County Coalition for the Homeless and Hungry. He provided current information on both the local and national scene. Finally, I had the pleasure of getting to know Bill Laney, (2008) author of *Homeless Isn't Hopeless: a Remarkable Journey of Hope and Humor*. Bill came to Gainesville for speaking engagements in which he both inspired us and debunked many stereotypes about homeless people. Bill's book is a highly readable account of his extraordinary experiences, on Greyhound buses, as a homeless man.

This book is also a product of the input from friends Anne Boches and Chris Flavin who read early manuscripts and provided insightful suggestions for improving the story and its continuity. Dr. Barbara Pace, who professed a childhood interest in mapmaking, constructed the sketch of the Ocklawaha River contained in one of the chapters.

Lastly, Dorie Stein urged me to follow Robinson's advice, and provided continuous and enthusiastic support of my efforts to complete this novel. And did I mention a cat named Dowsie? He respectfully sat on my desk, while I worked and kept me company on my imaginary journey through creek, river, homeless woman's campsite, and the many rehearsals at the Tuscawilla Theater.

Gainesville, Florida
October 2009

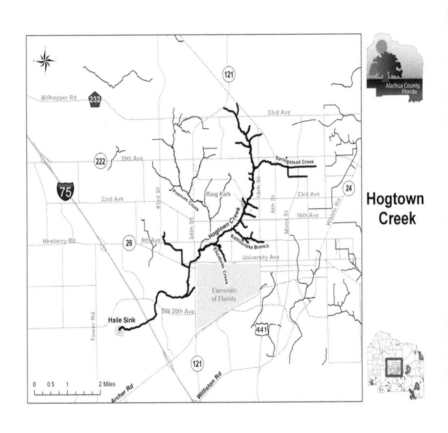

Hogtown Creek

Prologue

The two University of Florida students entered the Hogtown Creek from just north of the campus. The girl didn't want to use the Hogtown Greenway since she took pride in knowing other ways to access the creek. The pair half skidded down the fern- and ivy-covered slope on a bank lined with trees and shrubs—tall loblolly pines, sweetgums, hickories, and thick vines. Grabbing hold of saplings and bamboos helped them control their descent. Once at the bottom, standing on a low knoll next to the shallow sandy stream, they remained silent and looked around. The air smelled fresher below street level and there was less noise made by cars and motor scooters as students hurried to their classes.

The young man spoke first. "This is so cool. I can see why you love it here. It's almost a jungle right in the middle of the city."

"And instead of majoring in business," the girl replied, lightly punching his shoulder, "you could have a career exploring places like this instead of spending time in some stupid office."

It was a fresh spring morning in Gainesville, and the crisp air heightened the palette of green hues that enveloped them. The smothering north Florida humidity had not yet arrived. They listened to hear the chirp of a cardinal, hidden somewhere along the forested bank, and then looked up to see a pileated woodpecker boring holes in a nearby tree. Their attention slowly shifted from sounds of the city to those of the woods.

"It's like really amazing, isn't it?" said the young woman. She slapped at the mosquitoes biting her bare legs and wished she had worn jeans rather than shorts. "It's been here forever. My dad used to take us kids hiking in the creek to look for shark teeth and fossils. He told us we were on a limestone ridge formed millions of years ago as the whole region was rising out of the sea. Hard to imagine, huh?"

"Yeah, it still looks pretty primitive…except for the Blue Moon beer bottle over there on the bank."

11

"Ugh," she said. "I hate it that people throw their trash down here."

They stood watching the slow-moving water until the girl said, "C'mon, let's take off our flip-flops and walk the creek. It's easier to go barefoot. Besides, that's how you find fossils—with your toes. Oh, and be on the lookout for snakes and alligators." There was a glint of teasing on her face, but the boy didn't see it.

After removing his shoes, the young man hesitated, but she grabbed his hand and pulled him down the slope into the stream. The water was only a few inches deep and they splashed around in it, like children.

"Oh, don't worry about critters, city boy. I was only teasing. They won't bother you unless you step on one. Anyway, I haven't ever seen gators here or anything dangerous, for that matter."

She led the way and, as they walked along the streambed, she proudly pointed out some of the plants and trees along the bank. She was a botany major and eager to impress her new friend.

They walked in silence for a while, studying the sand for hidden treasures. Finding none, the boy casually glanced at the surrounding bank. "What's that pretty bush up there with the red berries? Bet the birds love it."

"Oh, that's one of the invasive plants—the coral ardesia," she replied.

"I know about invasive plants," he said. "We've got the Maleluca tree down in the Everglades. They say it's taking over everything."

"So, you're not ecologically challenged after all," she teased. "There are lots of exotics here, like the ivy and heavenly bamboo we saw coming down from the road."

"And don't forget the air potato," he said, stooping to dislodge a sharp object he felt with his foot. It was a pull tag from a drink can. He shrugged and put it in his pocket.

"How do you know about them?" she asked, walking just ahead of him.

"Oh, a friend of mine took me on an air potato roundup last semester."

12

"My dad used to nuke them."

"What?" He came up alongside her.

"Yeah. Daddy called himself an eco-terrorist. 'Course that was before being a terrorist was so...well, so terrifying," she laughed. "Anyway, he'd carry a can of herbicide or some homemade concoction and zap the invasive plants."

The boy considered the idea and concluded, "Sounds like a good plan. Did you decide to major in botany because of your dad?"

"I guess so. But it turns out that zapping the plants wasn't such a great idea now that we know so much about water pollution. All the bad stuff goes down the aquifer where we get our drinking water. In fact, this creek is pretty polluted. We're going to have to scrub our feet when we get back to the dorm."

"Hey," the young man said, "I think I just felt something hard. Wait a minute." He bent down, moved his fingers around in the sand, and picked up a small shark tooth. How cool is this?" he asked, showing his find to the girl.

"Awesome," she said. "Keep poking through the sand. Maybe you'll find some more."

They continued their slow walk searching the sandy creek bed. After a while, the boy asked, "So is it true that Gainesville was once named Hogtown?"

Before she could answer, the girl's attention was drawn to a large dark mound at the base of the concrete embankment ahead. At this distance, it looked like overstuffed bags of garbage dumped at the bank of the narrow stream. Yet there was something odd about it. "Look at that," she said, pointing toward the culvert. "What do you think it is?"

The students moved toward the heap until its shape became apparent.

"Oh, my God," the girl cried. "It's a body." She looked up at the road above. "Someone's fallen into the creek."

They sloshed through the shallow water toward the culvert, and soon arrived within feet of a large crumpled body. It looked like a man in blue jeans and a blue work shirt. He was lying face down, legs spread apart, torso half on the bank and half in the water. His head was twisted grotesquely, and his hair was matted with dried blood."

"Jesus," the boy cried, looking at the girl who stood transfixed and ashen. "Do you see that? His wrists are tied behind his back. Get your cell phone and call 911."

She reached into the pocket of her shorts, pulled out her phone, and pushed in the number.

"I think I'm going to be sick," the boy said. He waded to the bank, and started to retch.

Chapter 1

The Swamp was noisy, but not as crowded as it is during regular semesters. The restaurant is situated directly across from the University of Florida campus and shares its name with the Ben Hill Griffin Stadium. It's a favorite hangout for students and even the locals occasionally eat here. The food is good, reasonably priced, and the collegiate environment reminded us adults we were living in a college town.

The sport *du jour* blared from the large screen TVs situated around the main dining area, and the aroma of beer and grilled meat told me why it was Jeffrey who had suggested we lunch here. Though well beyond his undergrad years, it remained his milieu.

"God, I really missed you, Red," he said, taking my hand in his from across the table. "Gainesville isn't the same without the lovely Lorelei Crane. Right, Becky?"

Becky, who sat between us, smiled and nodded emphatically. Her shoulder length wiry hair bobbed as though electrified. She was in her mid-thirties, but still fit the collegiate mold. Perhaps it was because all of her friends were perpetual grad students or instructors at the local college.

I chuckled at Jeffrey's silly rhyme, withdrew my hand, and unfolded my place setting. He sat back in his chair, cocked his head, and gave me a wistful look, which made me uncomfortable. It suggested a bittersweet rendezvous of old lovers which, in his view, we always would be.

"I have been gone quite awhile," I said in a more detached tone than I intended. "Although at this moment it feels like I never left. It's great to see you both. Nothing much seems to have changed, except the traffic has gotten worse."

Becky said, "It's not just the traffic. Have you seen the new apartments around campus? Who's going to rent them all? Anyway,

Lorelei, we were afraid you'd never come back to Gainesville. Especially after we heard you sold your Micanopy house."

I felt warmed by Becky's concern. "What do they call it, 'the Gainesville suck?' Once you've lived here you just can't stay away from the place. I confess, I might have remained longer in South Florida if it weren't for Renee offering me such a juicy part in her fall production."

"How is your mother?" Becky asked. "You mentioned on the phone that she's in a retirement home down there."

"Oh, she's feisty as ever despite her stroke." I paused, not wanting to dwell on any particulars about my mother's saga. "But I really am glad to see you both. Catch me up on what's been happening this year. When I returned from Apalachicola, I didn't get to see you guys before I had to rush down south. When we talked on the phone you told me about your work, but what's been happening on the environmental scene?"

"Are you going to tell her?" Becky said, looking at Jeffrey.

He took a deep breath, pursed his lips, and was about to speak just as the server came to take our food orders and bring drinks. Jeffrey leaned forward and said, "Lor, you just wouldn't believe it. Practically the whole time you were gone we've been fighting the same damn old battles to keep development off of the Prairie. It just never stops."

Becky shot Jeffrey a quizzical look as though she were surprised by what he said in response to her question.

He continued, "First a whole new development, Cottage Grove, springs up—almost overnight—across from the Prairie on 441."

"Yes, I was shocked when I saw it while driving down to Micanopy. I went down to pick up some things from storage and visit our old cat, Maynard."

Becky put her hand on Jeffrey's arm and said, "Do you want me to tell her?"

"Tell me what?" I asked, sensing her urgency.

Jeffrey frowned and said, "Becky, how about let's ease Lorelei back into the scene. Just tell her about the Gainesville Country Club deal, and some of the other stuff that's been going on."

Becky shrugged, withdrew her hand, and said, "It was a real shocker. All of a sudden the old Gainesville Country Club started pushing plans to expand. They wanted to build umpteen condos right on the edge of the Paynes Prairie. Can you believe it? They even tried to convince everybody it would improve the Prairie. They must have thought we were stupid or something. Improve it with multi-story condos on the edge? Thank goodness the County Commission finally turned them down. But you know they or someone else will just try again."

"Well, I'm glad they put a stop to it," I said. I had a mental image of towering condos on the edge of all the serene beauty and wildlife on the open prairie. I loved driving across it, from Micanopy to Gainesville, and witnessing the change of seasons.

Becky continued, "And, on top of that, there's..." Her face became flushed with agitation as she outlined a litany of issues from water bottling plants at nearby springs to old grievances of gopher tortoises buried alive by developers. She had not lost her righteous passion about injustice to the land and to animals. I set my face in an interested look, but felt a sense of detachment as I studied my two friends.

Jeffrey tolerantly sat just staring out of the window during Becky's rant. He seemed calmer and less intense than I had known him to be. He's aging, I thought, and noticed he had acquired a sprinkling of gray at the temples of his dark curly hair. He still looked younger than his 43 years. His muscular and lean athletic build suggested he had been working out. I felt a familiar twinge of attraction to the man who had been my first husband. I studied Becky, and saw she had put on weight, which made her face look more mature. She appeared more womanly than the bright-eyed grad student with whom I once worked at the Center for Earth Options. And her professional costume must have changed from jeans and short tops to the smart slack suit she wore today.

Now that I had returned to Jeffrey's turf, I idly wondered what our relationship would be. I knew he and Becky had a brief affair, and that it ended amiably. With whom was he currently involved?

When Becky stopped talking to take a sip of water, Jeffrey turned to me. "You see, Lor? We could use your help. Can we count on you now that you're back?"

"Help with what exactly?" As if I didn't know the answer to my question. "Oh, c'mon you two. You can't be planning any of your eco-actions again. As I recall, Jeffrey, you were nearly killed, and some of your Earth Save cohorts were arrested the last time you played that game."

"You know what they say, Lor, 'what doesn't kill you outright makes you stronger.'" He gave me one of his innocent silly grins, as if it had all been a big joke.

The server reappeared with our sandwiches. I had my favorite, portobello mushroom quesadilla, Jeffrey had a cheeseburger and fries, and Becky raised her fork with relish as a large Greek salad was set down before her. The conversation stopped and, as though the mere presence of food caused a reflexive action on our part, we began to down our meals. We were all good eaters.

Finally, Jeffrey took a swig of beer, wiped his mouth, and said, "Lorelei, you know we can't just sit back and do nothing while North Florida is trashed by development like they've done down south. Too many of us have invested so much to protect it."

I raised my hands to ward off what I knew could be a full-length diatribe. "Listen, my dear friends, I'm definitely with you in spirit, but I've got a complicated play to prepare for, I've just moved into my new condo, and I'll need to make trips back down south to check on my mom. I don't have the extra time or energy to be involved with you guys. I'll be happy to write you a check, but that's about all I can do."

"Okay, okay," Jeffrey said. "Let's not talk about it right now. Maybe you'll feel different after you get settled into a routine. I assure you we're not going to do things the way we did before. We're a lot smarter now, and more careful."

I was relieved to be let off the hook so easily but, knowing Jeffrey, I knew it would be a temporary reprieve. He was nothing if not persistent.

In contrast to Jeffrey's attitude, Becky appeared upset by my response. She cast him a pleading look, and said, "But Jeffrey, we agreed we needed her help to find out…"

Jeffrey gave her a warning look that stopped her from finishing the sentence.

"Find out what?" I asked. "What is it with you two? What aren't you telling me?"

"Nothing important," he said, and changing the subject asked, "So tell us about the play you're in. Another classic?"

"Yes, it's *Sweeney Todd: the Demon Barber of Fleet Street*." I put on a ghoulish face and wrung my hands. "And if you can believe it, I'm going to be Mrs. Margery Lovett—maker of human meat pies."

Becky said, "The movie was so gory. It made me glad I was a vegetarian. Lorelei, that woman is so unlike you. How can you play someone so evil?"

"It's called acting, my dear," I said, repeating Olivier's famous retort. "But the truth is, it's a fun part, and I'm excited about it just because it is such a different role for me. I got bored playing the *Cherry Orchard* again. This one is part Dickens and part farce."

Pointing at me with his last french fry, Jeffrey said, "I didn't see the movie, but I know the play was a musical. I never pictured you in a singing role."

"Oh, Renee isn't doing the musical version. She's using the Christopher Bond script that was the source for Sondheim and Wheeler's musical. It's going to be a dramatic production."

"Anything you're in will be really cool," Becky said with a look of admiration. "I can't wait to see it."

We finished lunch. "My treat," I said, grabbing the check from the center of the table. "I've missed you all. Everything in South Florida felt so…well, so glitzy and frenetic. Even if I don't join your adventures, I hope we can spend time together."

"We will. Trust me," Jeffrey said. He stared at me for a moment. His coal black eyes held a searching look as though hoping to prompt some emotional response from me. He rose, bent down, kissed my cheek, and brushed his hand in my hair. "Oh, that gorgeous red hair. I'm so glad you're not coloring it anymore."

"Jeffrey," I protested, squirming a bit at his intimate gesture.

"No problem, Red. Thanks for lunch. I've got to get back to the Plant Lab. It's tough being the boss—you can't goof off like everybody else."

"Jeffrey a boss?" I teased. "Who would've pictured that?"

Becky made no response. Her eyes followed Jeffrey as he left the restaurant, and she continued staring in that direction even after walked out the door.

"What's on your mind, Becky? You're obviously worried about something."

She quickly turned toward me. "Well, I've been thinking about whether I should tell you. He didn't want me to, but…"

"Tell me what? For goodness sakes, get it out already."

Her eyes took on a glassy, frightened cast, and she shook her head to dispel the emotion.

"What is it Jeffrey didn't want you to tell me?"

"I guess, he thought we should wait a bit."

I was becoming more impatient. I bent closer and put my hand on hers. "Tell me right now," I urged in a soft voice.

Becky's eyes opened wide, and once again they held a hint of fear. "It's about the murder," she blurted out. "I'm really scared, Lorelei."

Chapter 2

"Murder?" I replied, stunned by Becky's announcement. "Who in heaven's name has been murdered?"

"Stoker, one of our Earth Save buddies. His real name is...was Adam Kincaid," she said, with a catch in her voice. "I don't even remember why we called him Stoker. But Lorelei, his death was so shocking and gruesome. They found him face down in Hogtown Creek."

"Stoker," I mused aloud. "A big burly guy with a coarse mouth? I think I met him at the Prairie rally a few years ago."

"Oh, Stoker just liked to shock people. He was a sweetheart when you got to know him."

"So, he drowned in the creek?"

"He didn't just drown. It looked like he'd been thrown there from the road—like some bag of garbage. His wrists were tied behind his back."

"When did all this happen?"

"Way before you got back in town—on Memorial Day weekend. Anyway, we're all upset. I mean we were with him like the night before they found him. There was this big beer party at Charley's. Stoker was already pretty smashed when the party broke up but they said he stayed till the bar closed. He really was such a good guy." Becky's eyes filled with tears.

"I'm so sorry," I said. "I know how much you care about your friends in Earth Save. I can only imagine how long it will take to get over Stoker's death—especially since he was murdered. How awful."

"That's just it, Lorelei. We can't find any peace about it until someone catches the murderer. We've got to know who killed him, and how it happened. It's driving us crazy. It's all me and my boyfriend can talk about."

"Your boyfriend?"

"Oh, Bear and I hooked up about a year ago. He's part Navaho Indian. I've learned so much from him about Indian culture and spirituality. We have the same beliefs about nature. I hope you get to meet him."

"He sounds interesting. So, about your friend Stoker, haven't the police been able to tell you anything?"

"That's just it. Gainesville police won't tell us about the investigation. All we know is what's on the news and in the newspaper."

"Hands tied behind his back? It doesn't sound like a mugging."

"Exactly what we thought," Becky said. "He left his car at Charley's, but we didn't think that was unusual. When Stoker got drunk he'd walk back to his apartment. He lived nearby."

"So you think someone picked him up while he was walking home? What did it say in the paper?"

Becky shrugged, and lifted her hands in a gesture of dismay. "Practically nothing, except they identified the body and suspected homicide. We wouldn't know any more than that, but it was one of Jeffrey's student lab assistants who found the body. She and a boyfriend were walking the creek, and just came up on poor Stoker. They saw him lying face down with his hands tied behind his back. They called 911, and were so scared they climbed up to the street to wait for the police."

"Poor kids," I said. "It must have been traumatizing."

"Yeah. The police told Jeffrey's student not to discuss what she saw with anyone. But of course she told Jeffrey about it."

The waiter returned with my receipt and credit card.

Becky glanced at her watch and stood. "Oh, I need to get going. I'm meeting with a computer consultant this afternoon."

"I still can't picture you working for a real-estate company," I said as we left the restaurant.

"I needed to make more money than the Center could pay, and I actually kind of like it. It's a break not to be around people trying to save the planet 24/7."

"I see your point," I said and put my arm in hers as we walked toward the parking lot. A troubled look returned to her face. "Now that you've told me about Stoker. What is it you and Jeffrey think I can do to help?"

"Lorelei, you have connections in the sheriff's office. Detective McBride knows about the investigation. They've questioned us about it, but they won't tell us what they've learned. We hoped you would find out what they know and kind of keep us posted. Some of us are very worried."

We arrived at her car, in the Gator Plaza parking lot. The sun's intense heat made me look around for a shady spot to continue the conversation. Seeing none, I stood there, feeling beads of perspiration begin at my temples and leak down the side of my face.

I said, "I understand why you're shocked over your friend's death. Murder is frightening. But what exactly is it you are worried about?" I asked.

She considered my question for a moment before responding. "Well, for one, Stoker was radical—even for us. When he was drunk, which was often, he'd get into people's faces about issues. Some of us are wondering if he got aggressive with the wrong people. You know, maybe talked too much with some rednecks or eco-vigilantes. Maybe even government undercover agents. Anyway, it's got us all nervous."

"Eco-vigilantes and undercover agents? It sounds a bit far-fetched," I said. "You really think someone murdered him because of something he said?"

"Or, something he might have done." Becky looked around and lowered her voice to a whisper. "They call us eco-terrorists and I call everyone who fights and hurts us, eco-vigilantes. Even though more and more people are talking about saving the environment, ever since 9/11 it's gotten more dangerous to be a real activist. You've heard of Tre Arrow, the anti-logging activist?"

"I think I remember reading about him. Mostly because he had such an interesting name and grew up in Florida."

Becky said, "The FBI arrested Tre, and he's been in prison here and in Canada for years. They even admitted that environmental activists were a top domestic terrorism priority. Can you imagine? Sure, we sometimes act a little crazy, like we're Edward Abbey's

"Monkey Wrench Gang," but we never kill anyone. The right-wing nuts don't mind killing people—like that Oklahoma City bomber. And what about murdering doctors who perform abortions? So, you might think it's silly for us to be so worried, but that's why we need to know about Stoker's murder. Is there someone out to get us, too?"

Suddenly I was reminded of the old adage "If you're not paranoid, you just don't understand what's going on."

"Okay, I get it," I said. "I was already planning to touch base with Homer McBride. I'll see what I can find out for you."

"Gee, thanks, Lorelei," she said, and gave me a quick hug. "Gotta rush now. It's great seeing you back in Gainesville."

"You too, Becky."

She got into her car and drove away. I walked over to Goering's Bookstore where I had parked when I picked up a copy of Robert Mack's book on Sweeney Todd.

I felt a sudden wave of melancholy when I returned to my condo. There were boxes everywhere, and it was impossible to place my furniture until I unpacked. The effort seemed huge. I plunked myself down on the side of the couch that was clear, and stared out of the window. At least I had a beautiful view of Lake Alice, I thought. The sunlight hit the pale green water and bounced off the surface like sparklers. Fortunately, from this distance I couldn't see the alligators which inhabited the lake. It made me think of the time Delcie and I stood on the bank, outside the Noodle Bowl restaurant, and I spied an alligator that seemed to be coming toward me. I have a morbid fear of these prehistoric creatures. Jeffrey liked to tease me about it just as my closest friend, Delcie, did on that day.

As if on cue, my cell phone rang and the familiar voice said, "So, girl, how long were you going to wait before calling me? You wanted me to help unpack when you got all your stuff out of storage."

"Gee, Del, you must be psychic. As always, you've called in the nick of time. I do need your help, and not just with my stuff. I feel so depressed."

"The trip down to Micanopy?"

"Yes, maybe that's it. And seeing all the things from my former life."

"Okay, as soon as I clear up some things this afternoon, I'll pick up Chinese and come over. Food always cheers you up."

I sighed, "Delcie Wright, you are…"

"Forget the superlatives, I know who I am. Get started unpacking, and before you know it, I'll be there. You got any wine?"

"I haven't had time to shop yet. Better bring some."

"Okay, darlin', Delcie's emergency actress rescue service will be there by 5 p.m."

"Bless you," I said, already feeling better.

True to her word, Delcie appeared at my door at a little after five o'clock. We hadn't been together since that Christmas Eve in Apalachicola. Come to think of it, that was another time I was feeling depressed. I was sitting alone in Sophie's café feeling sorry for myself when Delcie showed up—out of the blue. They say nobody can really rescue another person—except perhaps physically—but Delcie was the closest thing to my guardian angel.

"Jeez, what a mess," she said as she walked in the door carrying several bags. "You need some organization, girlfriend. Everything is everywhere. Where's the kitchen? I need to put this stuff down before I can give you a proper welcome back to Gainesville."

I pointed the way, and continued standing at the front door as she wove through the tower of boxes and furniture. Delcie was beautiful as ever. The way she moved her tall dancer's body and her creamy dark skin made her look elegant in everything she wore. Today, it was a white two-piece pantsuit with an expensive-looking turquoise silk blouse. Not your ordinary private investigator's outfit, I thought.

"Okay, dinner can be ready whenever we are," she said, returning to where I stood. "I freed the microwave from its box."

We hugged and I started giggling.

"What're you laughing about? I thought you were depressed." She stepped back to better appraise me. "Hey, look at you. You got a fine tan down there in Miami."

"Ft. Lauderdale."

"Whatever. Keep up the suntan and we'll be able to pass for sisters."

"Nothing would please me more than to be your sister," I said, and placed my arm next to hers to compare the depth of our skin tone. Hers was darker.

"So, how's Mama? She adapting to her new home?" Delcie walked over to the large windows and looked out at the lake.

"More or less," I said, sitting down on the couch. "She was pretty angry about selling the house. I didn't like to do it, either. But we both realized she couldn't live alone anymore, and live-in help is too damn expensive."

"Don't I know it," Delcie said, coming over to join me. "I've got an auntie in Georgia who's just been put into a nursing home. Lord, the family hated to do it but…well, you know."

"Mom's situation made me think about what's going to happen to me when I get old and sick. I don't think they have retirement homes for actors anymore. Anyway, at least mom has friends at the care center, and it's a beautiful facility with lots of activities. She's in good hands. Now, c'mon, let's talk about something else before I put you to work."

"Well, if it's talkin' were doing, let me get that bottle of Merlot I brought. Do you have any glasses unpacked?"

"Just a couple of water glasses. They're on the sink."

Delcie returned from the kitchen, poured the wine, and we clinked glasses. We sipped the wine and gazed out the windows as the sun began its descent.

"Nice view," she said. "But are you gonna miss that beautiful home of yours in Micanopy? It was so peaceful there."

"I don't know. I wouldn't feel comfortable there without Bill. It's strange, between selling the Micanopy house, and my childhood home—all in the same year—there's no place where I have a history. You know what I mean?"

"I think I do. But it can be a good thing, can't it?"

"Probably," I said, taking another sip of wine. "I guess you could say letting go of the past is liberating—you know, a fresh start. On the other hand, it's a bit daunting. Speaking of the past, I had lunch with Becky and Jeffrey today."

"What's happening with them?"

"Oh, mostly same old. I'll tell you about it later."

"Let's get back to your fresh start idea. You actors are always movin' around anyway. Look at it from this angle, now life's given you the chance to explore new territory. Isn't that artistic fodder?" It was Delcie's characteristic bit of pragmatism.

"You're right. I've got to stay positive," I said and sat up straighter.

Delcie mused, "Did you ever think of going back to New York or out West?"

"Oh, yes, but I need to stay around here for a while—you know, for Mother's sake. And Gainesville will do for the time being. At least the play's going to be fun."

"Well, I'm glad you're back. I missed you."

I patted her arm and felt a surge of affection for my old friend. "Thanks. So, how about you? When we talked on the phone you always sounded busy and rushed. I assume the PI business is flourishing?"

"You assume right. I've even had to hire an assistant—since you wouldn't take the job. I still say you'd make a terrific investigator. Look how you helped solve those murders in Wakulla Springs."

"Oh, that was a trip. Even Homer complimented me about my investigative skills. And, speaking of Homer, have you had any contact with him lately?"

She thought a moment. "Let's see, last time I saw McBride was during a court case about two months ago. I was working for the defense. When I said hello outside the courtroom, he was his usual patronizing self. It felt so good when his sorry white ass got whopped by our lawyer. Forgive me, Lorelei."

I waved away her apology. I wasn't surprised by the comment. I knew Delcie had an underlying anger toward white law enforcement officers. I didn't blame her, really. She had encountered her share of prejudice, and probably still did.

Delcie said, "So, I take it you haven't talked to him? The two of you seemed to be getting so close last year."

Close just about described the extent of my relationship with Homer McBride. I had a sudden image of the two of us after the final meeting at the Wakulla Springs Lodge, standing outside the building and shivering in the cold. When we parted, there was one of those sparks between us that made me sure he was going to kiss me. He didn't, and I had to admit my relationship with Homer McBride was all sparks, no fire.

"No, I haven't heard from him. I guess absence didn't make his heart grow fonder," I said. "We both had busy lives. Anyway, so far as I know, he's still married. And, he's the loyal type."

"The loyal type? More like the not-yours type."

Chapter 3

The next morning, I awoke and lay in bed half dreaming about Homer McBride. I pictured him in the navy corduroy jacket, red plaid shirt, and jeans which he wore at Wakulla Springs that last day. I remember thinking how attractive and manly he looked. There could be a relationship, but my ambivalence returned, and I wondered what it would be like to see him again.

Surveying the large airy bedroom, I dreaded the sight of all the unpacked boxes that lined the walls. Delcie and I didn't talk much while we were unpacking last night. But around about midnight, we got giddy and had some wild moments when the reggae music on a cable station captured us. We broke into a dance and collapsed on the couch in hysterical laughter. It reminded me of Saturday nights in our college dorm room. By that point in the evening, we knew we were both too tired to continue working and Delcie left.

Earlier, I told her about my lunch with Jeffrey and Becky. I asked her about the Hogtown Creek murder. She said all she knew about it was the brief newspaper account, and was surprised to learn the victim was a friend of Becky and Jeffrey's.

She echoed Becky's concern by saying, "Let's not be naïve, Lorelei. There're a lot of folks around here who think it's the environmentalists—the 'anti's' they call them—who're keeping people from using their land like they want to, and blocking economic growth. And things are startin' to get ugly with the fighting over our water supply. Maybe you haven't heard, but Central Florida wants water piped down from the rivers up here. You just wait and see…there'll be shotguns coming out over this."

I didn't want to think about Delcie's grim predictions, so I got out of bed, placed my yoga mat in front of the bedroom windows, and did a set of postures. I focused on the lake and surrounding woods.

The view was almost as soothing as the one I had from my bedroom deck in Micanopy.

I showered, and took a long look at myself in the mirror. At forty-eight, my body was ample but still shapely. Of course I had the advantage of height—5'7"—and a mane of red hair, which seemed to serve as a distraction from any imperfections. In spite of my love of food, I managed to keep myself in good shape by doing yoga and working out. I had kept my membership in the Gainesville Health & Fitness Center. I knew, once I started back at the theater, I would have to resume my former exercise regimen.

After breakfast, of leftover Chinese vegetables and rice, I punched in Homer McBride's work number. He didn't answer, so I left a message asking him to call me.

Within an hour, the cell phone rang and I answered, "Homer?"

He responded, "You sound breathless. Did you just come in?"

"Oh, no, I was unpacking, and had to track down the phone. Thanks for calling back so soon."

"No problem. It's good to hear your voice, Lorelei. I always meant to call but... Anyway, I read that the Tuscawilla is putting on a play with you in the lead. When did you get into town?"

"Just a few days ago. I'm living downtown now. In a condo. I sold my house in Micanopy."

"Good. Maybe we'll get to see each other."

"That's why I called. I wonder if I could see you sometime soon? There's something I want to talk to you about—in person."

"Sounds mysterious. Yes, I've got about an hour free this afternoon. I'll be down at the courthouse. Can you meet me at Maude's about two o'clock?"

"Yes, I'll see you then. Thanks, Homer," I said, surprised to feel butterflies in my stomach at the prospect of seeing him again.

I sat on the edge of the bed, and stared at the cell phone in my hand. I realized I was now fully reconnected to my old past. The pleasure I felt talking with Homer gave way to a sinking feeling like the one you have when the doctor tells you your tests came our fine…except for one. My life here was déjà vu despite the new acting role and new place to live. For me, Gainesville held complicated relationships, memories, and the experience of loss. By contrast, life in South Florida had been so simple—work and caring for my mother. Had I made a mistake by returning?

I arrived at Maude's and found a table outside, under an umbrella, in the far corner of the little plaza. Homer showed up within a few minutes, and I stood to give him a hug. He held me for several moments in a surprisingly warm embrace.

"It's good to see you again, Lorelei. I've missed you," he said.

We sat down, and I looked at him closely. He seemed unsettled, even nervous, which was surprising for him.

"What's wrong, Homer?"

He looked around for a waiter and, seeing none, stood up again. "Let me get us some drinks and we'll talk. I just have an hour before I have to get on the road. What'll you have?"

I asked for a latte, and watched him walk toward the interior of the coffee house. He was only couple of inches taller than me, his compact build suggested manly strength, and he looked as sexy as ever.

He returned with the drinks, and pulled his chair next to mine. "To your return," he said raising his mug of coffee in a toast before sipping it.

"You said you had to get on the road?"

"I'm driving up to see my son in Atlanta. He's been there with his mother since school let out. Usually he stays with me for the second half of the summer." A frown momentarily crossed his face. He asked, "And your mother? How is she doing?"

"She had a small stroke. I helped her move her into a retirement village, and sell her house—our house. My folks had lived there forever. It was tough," I said.

He nodded, and sipped his coffee. "So you're going to be in *Sweeney Todd*? I saw the movie. It was too dark and bloody for my taste."

"Too dark and bloody? And that from a homicide detective?"

He gave me a rueful smile. "Yeah, I guess I just see too much of it in real life."

31

He moved his chair back, heaved a deep sigh, and seemed caught up in his own thoughts. The energy between us shifted as though a cloud had passed over and darkened our spirits.

"What is going on, Homer? You're not your usual…how shall I put it, edgy self."

Silently, he seemed to debate whether or not to answer my question. At last he said, "Bobby's mother—my wandering wife—has decided we should divorce. I think she's been shacking up with some fellow FBI agent. Anyway, she told me she's going to file, and she wants us to tell the boy about it together. That's why I'm going to Atlanta."

Hmm, I thought. I had only a hunch about Homer's relationship with her, but I knew how painful it was to divorce.

"I'm so sorry, Homer. I'm sure you're worried about the impact on your son."

"Yeah, it might be tough on him. Though his life won't change too much," he admitted, and reflectively looked at his watch.

I could see he was anxious to get on the road. I didn't want to seem callous about his situation, but knew our time together was very short.

I said, "I had lunch with Jeffrey Waterman and Becky yesterday. Becky is very worried about the murder of her friend, Adam Kincaid. Can you tell me anything about the case?"

"Now, Lorelei, we're assisting the Gainesville Police Department on this case. We've been interested in Kincaid since long before the murder, but even if it was totally ours…"

I expected his response. On the way over, I had planned my strategy. "Yes, I know you can't talk about an ongoing investigation. But I might be able to help with the investigation. Kincaid was one of the activists at the rally we organized to stop the Valdez development. Remember? It was when I first met you, while I was working for the Center for Earth Options. I still know quite a few people in the environmental community. I might be able to get information that you can't get."

He cocked his head, and eyed me with a thoughtful expression. "Don't tell me you want to go sleuthing again. Even with a new play and all?"

"It wouldn't take much time or effort to ask some questions, and I might just turn up something missed by the police. You once told me I was pretty good at the getting information. So, what do you say?"

He finished his coffee and slid the mug to the center of the table before taking a pack of cigarettes out of his inside suit jacket. He removed a cigarette and tapped it on the tabletop in a typical stalling tactic. He caught my look of disapproval, and said, "I know, I know. I'm quitting as soon as they raise the price a dollar more a pack."

He lit the cigarette, exhaled, and I watched as the smoke curled upward in the still air. "Okay, I'll accept your offer on the Kincaid case. You probably can help us. But you have to swear not to disclose what I tell you. If too many details get out, it could hamper the investigation."

"I swear," I said, mentally crossing my fingers in the childish gesture negating a vow.

He looked around to be sure no one was in earshot, and said, "The first thing you should know is that Kincaid was executed."

"Executed?" I felt a shiver at the power of the word. "It makes me think of gangs and political assassins."

"You're not far off. In the last couple of weeks, a High Springs environmental activist was murdered, a Marion County commissioner who's taken a hard-line on water issues has been getting death threats—and now this case." He pursed his lips thoughtfully. "The events may not be linked, but it's possible some individuals—or group—is out to get the attention of the environment crowd."

I stared at him, in shock, and finally asked, "You say Kincaid was executed?"

"Gunshot to the head, hands tied behind his back, dumped over a land bridge into the creek. What do you think?"

So Becky's feeling of danger was not so far-fetched, after all.

"Have you warned any of the environmental groups? I'm especially concerned about Becky and her friends," I said.

"No, I don't want a panic. Like I said, the incidents may not be linked."

"But shouldn't they at least be aware of your suspicion?"

"If they read the newspaper, they can draw their own conclusions. The detectives aren't ready to go public with anything that can't be proven. Anyway, Kincaid's friends have been questioned, but they're a pretty tight-lipped group—not too friendly to cops. Frankly, there's not been much progress in the investigation."

His comment made me recall how antagonistic Becky was to McBride, years ago, when he tried to interview her at the Center.

"Maybe that's where I come in. I think they'd trust me."

"I figured as much," he said. "You could use your talent for getting information, and let me know what you learn from the tree huggers hotline. I'm sure Becky what's-her-name..."

"Haimovitz," I said.

"And, your friend Waterman will help. Maybe you can find out what this Kincaid fellow was up to that got him murdered."

"Okay, I'll try," I said, surprised by the enthusiasm I heard in my voice. I guess I did relish the chance to do some detective work.

Homer stood. He looked down at me with affection, and said, "Sorry, Lorelei, I've got to go. But I'll be back in a few days. Maybe we could have dinner together."

I touched the sleeve of his jacket, and replied, "That would be nice, Homer. I'll wait to hear from you."

I continued sitting at the table, and watched him disappear from view. I wondered how to warn Becky and Jeffrey about Homer's suspicions without sending Becky into a full panic. I also wondered about Adam Kincaid. What was he up to? And, was it something in which Becky and Jeffrey were also involved?

I left Maude's. On the way home, I decided to refocus my attention on tomorrow. It would be our first meeting at the theater, and I needed a clear head. The mystery of Adam Kincaid's death would have to wait. It was the other murders—those in *Sweeney Todd*—that demanded my immediate attention.

Chapter 4

It was Thursday, the day of the "meet and greet." As I headed down South Main Street to the Tuscawilla, I was looking forward to getting back to work and meeting the rest of the cast. Fortunately, after an intense workout at the fitness center, I had successfully pushed away thoughts about Homer, Becky and Jeffrey. All of that drama had to be put on hold until later.

I walked through the oversized glass doors of the theater, and took a deep breath. My first day in a new production was always the same—a tingling of emotion and awe when I first entered the house. For me, it was a spiritual experience not unlike that of visiting a cathedral, or other sacred space. The theater was the home of my passion.

The slightly musty odor combined with the faint smell of Florida pine was familiar. I looked around with renewed appreciation for the old building, a renovated lumber yard warehouse, to see shafts of sunlight streaming through the tall windows and landing at the foot of the well-worn tiger oak church benches which lined the walls.

I walked past the box office window to the small wine bar at the back of the lobby. The wall behind the bar held photographs of the actors who played in our company. The photos were artfully displayed and I was pleased with the shot they had of me. It was taken when I played Madame Ranevskaya in Chekhov's *The Cherry Orchard*. I rather liked seeing myself with dyed black hair and in nineteenth-century costume. Styles were so elegant then.

"Lorelei?"

I turned to discover Cassie Woodruff hurrying toward me. We hugged, and clung to one another like old friends at a high school reunion. Cassie was the young actress who played my sister in *The Cherry Orchard*. We immediately began exchanging personal updates

35

as we walked into the rehearsal hall and found seats next to each other.

Other cast members drifted in and sat at the long table. The murmur of conversations stopped the moment Renee Scalia, the Director, entered the room She was dressed in black and her hair was also dyed black. The former New York actress probably wouldn't be described as pretty, but she had finely chiseled features, a pale complexion, and cool blue eyes. Though petite in stature, she was like a Rottweiller in a Chihuahua's body—her presence commanded respect. Renee had the ability to either chill you to the bone with the briefest glance or comment, or wrap you in the warmth of her smile.

She greeted each person as she walked alongside the table. Pausing next to my chair, she said, "Lorelei Crane, how wonderful to see you back." I half stood up to receive her greeting, and she air kissed both my cheeks. "Everyone, Lorelei is one of our favorite actors. She's been away from us for too long. Watch and learn from her."

As I sat down, I thought, ye gads...*learn from her*? Now I'm the actor's doyenne? Yet, it was high praise from Renee and, as I looked around, I realized there was more than the usual complement of university theater majors. Cost saving, I guessed. Though, I knew from past experience, some of them were more talented than the seasoned actors with whom I had worked. There were also a couple of older men. It seemed apparent which one of them would play opposite me in the role of Sweeney Todd. Not bad looking, I thought.

"Now to business," Renee said. "Rick Warren is Stage Manager for this production. As some of you know, Chester moved back to Chicago. Fortunately, he recommended Rick who had worked with him at the Steppenwolf. Rick will go over the housekeeping details, and then I'd like you to introduce yourselves."

Rick, a middle-aged former-actor type, went through numerous items—rehearsal schedules, contact sheets, and the like. During the round of introductions, some of the actors shyly described their acting credentials; others made a joke of their experience, and the two obviously youngest actors enthusiastically admitted to this being their first-time in a professional acting company.

Finally, the man who would play Sweeney Todd identified himself as Jeremy Hastings, and made a modest introduction. I was struck by his physical appearance, which reminded me of another Jeremy—Jeremy Irons, the British actor.

"I've played some off-Broadway venues, regional theaters like this one, and a couple of road-show productions," he said, in a soft but pleasing voice. "You can see I've been around the block a time or two. Anyway, I look forward to getting to know everyone."

I was impressed. Especially since I had actually seen him perform, at the old Coconut Grove Playhouse, in a production of *Guys and Dolls*. He was multi-talented and looked to be a man in his forties who had kept up his physical appearance. He had a tall slender build, a classically handsome face with dark features, and a full shock of well-cut brown hair. I liked it that he listened attentively to all of the introductions, and nodded a friendly hello to me when I finished mine. Yes, I would enjoy getting to know Jeremy.

When the introductions were done, Renee said. "You are a talented group of actors, and I expect us to have a great production. Now, let's take a break before talking about the script." She looked at her watch, and added, "Equity Actors should stay in the room and meet with Rick. We'll give you an extra ten minutes."

Rick's meeting about our contracts was very efficient and left us about 10 minutes of break time. As I started out of the rehearsal room, I felt the cell phone vibrate in the pocket of my slacks. I took it out to see who was calling. It was Jeffrey.

I flipped open the phone. "Jeffrey, I'm in rehearsal," I said, feeling annoyed at the interruption.

"Won't take a minute, Lor. Can you take a bathroom break?"

"I'm on break now. Wait till I get out in the lobby."

I walked into the lobby with the phone to my ear. As I glanced sideways, I noticed Jeremy starting toward me. He stopped when he saw the phone.

"All right, what's on your mind?" I said, sitting down in a far corner of lobby.

"Did you get anything from Detective McBride?"

"What do you mean?"

"C'mon, Lor, Becky told me she talked to you about Stoker. She said you'd pump McBride for information about the case."

"What makes you think I've already talked with him?" I continued feeling irked by Jeffrey's call.

"Intuition. I know you had something going on with him," he said, pausing for my reaction. I didn't take the bait, and he continued, "When the two of you were there, in Apalachicola. It figured you'd call him as soon as you got back into town. Didn't you?"

Jeffrey always made assumptions about my relationships with other men and, what irritated me about it, he was usually right

"Yes, if you must know, we had coffee together yesterday afternoon."

"I thought so," he said in a satisfied tone.

"It's not what you're thinking, Jeffrey."

"Not my business, Red. But Becky and I are eager to know if you learned anything about Stoker? Did you?"

"I don't want to talk about it on the phone here. Yes, I did get some information."

"Great. When can I see you? I've got an Earth Save meeting tonight, but maybe we could meet for a pizza at Charley's, before the meeting. How about it?"

I thought for a moment before responding. Charley's Bar and Billiards had long been the hangout for Jeffrey and his friends. It was where he used to take me when we were dating and where, a few years ago, he guilt tripped me into getting involved with him in his treacherous scheme to disrupt development on Paynes Prairie. Jeffrey Waterman and I had history at Charley's. I was reluctant to open old memories, but I knew I had to warn him and enlist his help in the investigation.

"Okay, I'll meet you at Charley's. What time?"

"The meeting's at seven. Can you make it by six? That'll be enough time for us to talk."

"Yes," I said. "I'll see you then."

I closed my phone, and looked around to see some of the actors standing near the bar looking at the photographs, while others had gone outside to smoke. Neither Jeremy nor Cassie was in sight. I was glad, because I wanted a few minutes to think about my meeting with Jeffrey.

I wondered how I could find out what Stoker might-have-been into that resulted in his death. In a flash, I realized how to do it. I'd persuade Jeffrey to take me with him to the Earth Save meeting. I was confident members of the group would be more open with me than they had been with the authorities. It was with good reason, I thought, since some of their activities were illegal. As Becky pointed out, these were not good times to be involved in anything that could be classified as terrorism—ecological or otherwise.

After the break, we made our way through the first reading of the script which took about two hours. When we finished the last line, Renee asked,

"Well, what do you think of *Sweeney Todd: the Demon Barber of Fleet Street*?"

"He's a bloody maniac. By today's standards he'd be called a serial killer," said one of the young actors and looked around the table for affirmation.

Renee gave a nod of appreciation for the actor's directness, and turned to Jeremy. "What do you think, Mr. Todd? Are you a serial killer?"

Jeremy sat back, and thoughtfully steepled his fingers to his lips before responding. "In the strictest sense I may be, but is Hamlet a serial killer? No, from what I've read, Mr. Bond's script treats Sweeney Todd as a sympathetic character. After all, don't you think any man would be enraged against a judge who unfairly sends him to prison, then rapes his wife, and plans to seduce his young daughter? Isn't that enough to drive someone mad—exactly how Todd ends up."

"I think we'll be walking a tightrope with this play," I said. "As Jeremy suggested, one could read it as a classical drama. But Bond specifically says, in his subtitle, that it's a melodrama—you know the kind of play with background music to intensify the effects, like the old silent movies."

Renee said, "Melodrama, horror, and farce—at least as it's been played since George Dibdin-Pitt's original production in 1847. When C.G. Bond came along, in 1973, he produced an entirely new rewrite of the play—it's the one upon which Stephen Sondheim and all the others have based their productions."

The other "older man" in the group, Alexander Champion, gave a slight cough before speaking. He was to play the wicked Judge Turpin. Champion had a Dickensian look. He was in his sixties, had a pale and slightly pinched face, gray hair and goatee. He spoke in an affected cultured voice.

He said, "Last year, I saw the re-scored musical version at the American Conservatory Theater in San Francisco. It was pure magic. The actors remained on the stage for the whole production, and each one not only sang but played at least one instrument. Melodrama, or not, it was a very engaging experience." He added with a twinkle in his eyes, "I admit to being rather jealous of those multi-talented performers. I couldn't have done it."

Renee said, "You're quite right, about the production, Alex. John Doyle's direction was excellent. The play and actors were nominated for several Tony Awards in 2005-2006."

"I'm sorry to have missed the Broadway production with Patti Lupone—she played the tuba and percussion as Mrs. Lovett, can you just imagine?" said Champion, looking in my direction.

Renee responded, "Yes, I saw it and it was wonderful. In the original Bond script, the one we're using, he treats the characters with depth and the situation with a reality based in society at that time. The historical context is worth noting and you've got a handout about it. Briefly, it is one of societal turmoil and violence when it's more common for people to be murdered and to disappear. Bond also acknowledged borrowing from other dramas, such as the *Count of Monte Christo*."

One of the young actors looked troubled by Renee's comments, and said, "I get the violent times, and Todd's rage at what happened to him, but he starts murdering at random, doesn't he?" He looked at me and added, "His relationship with Mrs. Lovett and her meat pies. What's that about?"

The young woman sitting next to him shivered, and added, "The pies were made with the meat of people he killed. Like freaky."

The actor continued, "To me, it's more like a slasher movie than anything else. Wouldn't it be more honest if we played it tongue in cheek, rather than as a straight drama?"

Renee's face darkened slightly. I knew she was restraining herself from a sharp response for the challenge to her directorial conception. Patiently, she looked around the table for someone else to reply.

Cassie leaned forward, and gave the actor a reassuring smile before responding. She knew what trouble an innocent question like his could bring from a director like Renee.

"Yes, the whole murdering chair business and the human pies are pretty gruesome, but it's also a story of genuine human passion. For example, Sweeney Todd wants desperately to rescue and reconcile with my character, his daughter, Johanna. And she wants to escape the threat of marriage to someone she despises to run off with the man she loves. As Lorelei said, those are classic human dimensions, don't you think? And the tragic ending—why it's Shakespearean. I just love it."

The young man appeared unconvinced, and slumped down in his chair, seemingly aware that he shouldn't advance his opinion any further.

"Well then," Renee concluded, "we'll be talking more about all of this as we begin rehearsals. Perhaps, you'll have additional insights after you've reviewed the history of the play which is summarized in one of Rick's handouts. Now there's time for you to set-up your appointments for costumes. Once again, I'm excited to be working with all of you on this fascinating drama. See you tomorrow."

Renee waved goodbye to the cast and made her exit trailing a wake of other staff members who had recently drifted into the hall.

I checked my watch to see I had only enough time to get home for a quick change of clothes before meeting Jeffrey at Charley's. The slinky Chico's ensemble I was wearing wouldn't do for the Earth Save crowd. Jeans and an old shirt would be a more credible costume. I said goodbye to Cassie and some of the others. I made the appointment for my first costume fitting and was out the door with an hour to spare. Tonight, I would be in my secondary acting role.

Chapter 5

Some things really never do change. It was my thought as I pushed through the door into the cave-like atmosphere that was Charley's. It was a more or less typical neighborhood joint with a long bar, a loud jukebox, dark wooden booths around the perimeter of the room, and two large billiard tables in the middle. It took me a moment to adjust to the dim lighting, but I caught Jeffrey waving to me from a corner booth. I walked over and slid in opposite him.

"How'd your rehearsal go?" he asked, and took a sip from a bottle of beer.

"Pretty good for a first meeting. We've got some actors with great experience, and a bunch of young'uns. It's a good mix. I think it'll work. And you? What are you up to, Dr. Waterman?"

"Oh the usual, documenting and saving plant species. Sometimes I don't even know why I bother since the planet's going down the tubes."

"Oh, don't be so gloomy, Jeffrey. There's still hope."

"Really? I'm not as sanguine as you are, Red. We homo saps are pretty much devastating the whole bloomin' onion." He took another sip, put on one of his fakey smiles, and added, "Speaking of onions, what do you feel like? I'd better put in our order so we'll be finished in time for my meeting."

"Anything's fine for me. Thank goodness I don't have to diet for this role. Get me whatever you're having and some half sweet tea."

He got up and went to the bar to order. I looked around the room and was reminded of the last time I met him here. We had ordered a pizza but, by the time it came, Jeffrey had made me so angry, I walked out. He caught up with me, and we wound up eating the pizza, on the fender of his truck, along Highway 441. He then talked me into going with him to scout the site for a protest rally. Jeffrey always seemed to have ulterior motives. It made me uneasy to think, once again, my attempts to help Jeffrey might have unforeseen consequences.

He returned and slid back into the booth. "Okay, here's your tea. We're having burgers and sweet potato fries. It'll be here shortly." He leaned across the table, looked at me with his piercing dark eyes and, in a conspiratorial tone, said, "So, what did you learn from McBride?"

"I'll tell you, but first I want to make a bargain with you."

"Dammit, Lorelei, just tell me."

His outburst startled me. "Take it easy," I said, reaching across the table to pat his hand. "I'll tell you. Though he made me promise to keep it to myself. The gist of it is Homer thinks there may be some conspiracy to…well, intimidate and harm environmental activists."

"Harm? I'd called murder pretty extreme harm," he said, nervously drumming his fingers on the table. "Is that all your brilliant detective had to say?"

"No, apparently there was an environmental activist in High Springs who was killed recently."

"Yeah, I heard it was an accident. But you said 'killed.' Did McBride tell you the guy was murdered? Like Stoker?"

"No, he didn't give me details. He also told me a commissioner in Ocala is getting death threats. Homer thinks there might be a connection between those incidents and your friend's murder."

Jeffrey leaned back against the booth, let out an audible sigh, and said, "Jesus, Lorelei, if McBride has reason to suspect a connection—we're all in deep shit."

"I'm afraid for you, Jeffrey. And for Becky. That's why I agreed to help Homer."

"Help him how?"

"I want you to take me with you to the Earth Save meeting tonight. I told Homer I'd try to find out what some of the members know about Stoker's death. They've been very guarded with police investigators and so…" I shrugged at the obvious conclusion.

"That's the bargain? You want me to help you spy on our group—for McBride?" He shot me a look of disbelief.

"Not spy, you jerk. I want to help him figure out if someone's after you. Your friends may have important information and not even know it."

The bartender brought over our sandwiches, and Jeffrey said, "Let me think about it."

We both started eating. When I glanced at the bar, there was a chunky middle aged man in a plaid shirt that seemed to be staring at me. It didn't bother me since vanity allowed me to believe I was someone worth more than a fair share of men's glances.

My attention returned to Jeffrey who, having finished his hamburger, washed it down with the rest of his beer, and let out a loud belch.

"Sorry, Lor. I've been doing that a lot lately. I guess it's stress. Look, in the past, we've had members of our group arrested, fired from their jobs, even threatened by developer's thugs, but never anything like this."

"Still we don't know for sure what happened," I said, wanting to allay some of Jeffrey's anxiety. "McBride could be wrong. Maybe Stoker got into something else like a drug deal, or something."

"Unlikely. He was far too paranoid and cautious to mess with bad dudes."

"Well, whatever," I said. "Don't you agree with McBride that members of your group might know more than they were willing to tell the authorities? Please, just let me go to the meeting with you."

He studied me for a moment trying to make up his mind. "Okay, I'll bring you along, but I don't want you to give them the heebie jeebies. Everybody's upset enough about Stoker. Nobody even talks about him anymore—like it never happened. Anyway, don't even hint at what McBride told you. Let's approach this thing carefully."

"Fine," I said. "I agree. I'll just listen, and try to get a sense about who to talk with."

"You already know some of them so it shouldn't be a big deal to bring you along."

"Remind them I used to work for the Center for Earth Options," I said.

"Yeah, and you should give'em a story about being in South Florida and how it's radicalized you. Tell them you want to join Earth Save to keep the developers from making Gainesville into another Miami or Orlando."

"Wait a minute, I didn't say I actually wanted to join the group."

"Why not?" he said. "Isn't that what McBride wants—a mole?"

"But Jeffrey, I didn't plan to go that far."

"Besides," he held up a hand, ignoring my protest, and flashed a seductive look. "The bonus is, it'll give me a chance to see you more often. C'mon, Lorelei. You're up for a bit of adventure, aren't you?"

Old alarm bells sounded whenever Jeffrey challenged me to an adventure. The last time he seduced me into following him, I nearly died on a stormy night on Paynes Prairie. Before that, Jeffrey's version of adventure had included alligator encounters, near drowning on a white water raft, and numerous camping disasters. It was a dance going all the way back to the time before we married. But Jeffrey had the same effect on others. He was a natural leader or an instigator— sometimes I didn't know which—and people tended to get caught up in his schemes.

"Okay, I'll pretend to join your merry band of troublemakers. But don't expect me to go on any trick or tricking with you all."

"Naturally, I wouldn't expect my lovely Lorelei to put her sandals in the mud."

He looked up at the wall clock—it was almost seven—and slid to the edge of the booth. "Let's go. I'll get the check."

I once again noticed the man at the bar staring at me again then quickly looking away when we made eye contact. As Jeffrey stood, I touched his sleeve and said, "There's a guy at the bar who's been watching me. He's wearing jeans and a green plaid shirt."

Jeffrey glanced toward the bar, and said, "Oh him, I've seen him before. Kind of a doofus. Charley told me he comes into town to go to the VA. Anyway, Lorelei, don't you know by now that a gorgeous redhead like you is someone guys like to look at?"

"Maybe," I said, sliding out of the booth, but I had an uncanny feeling that the man's gaze was something more than admiring. "I'm going to the ladies' room. Wait for me. I'll be out in a couple of minutes, and I don't want to walk into the meeting by myself."

When I returned from the ladies' room, I looked for the chubby man at the bar, but he was gone. Jeffrey was waiting for me and led the way into the back room. It was the unofficial Earth Save group headquarters. Charley himself was a Vietnam vet and had a chip on his shoulder where any authority was concerned. The war and his treatment afterward had inoculated him against believing representatives of bureaucracies in general—governmental or corporate. His bar was a perfect fit for a gathering of radicals.

The back room was partially lined with stock, but it was large enough to hold a beaten-up old Ping Pong table which—without the netting—served as a meeting table. There were an assortment of chairs, a free-standing chalkboard, and a map of Alachua County which hung on a wall near the back door. The fluorescent lighting was softened by the soft glow of a cheap imitation Tiffany lamp which hung over the table. It was similar to the ones that hung over the pool tables in the bar. Charley must have gotten a deal on them, I thought.

When we entered, I saw several men seated against the wall, chairs tipped back, and drinking beer. They greeted Jeffrey and gave me a once over. I didn't know them. Jeffrey introduced me as his ex-wife, and said I'd be sitting in on the meeting. The men simply nodded in response.

"Sit here, Red," Jeffrey said, pulling a chair up to the table for me. "We'll be starting as soon as a few others arrive. Becky should be here pretty soon." He walked over to talk to the men, but I couldn't hear what he was saying.

"Lorelei? I never thought I'd see you here."

The greeting was from a longtime friend of Jeffrey's. He was a landscape architect who had often been a dinner guest at our house.

I stood up and we hugged. "Tim, how great to see you. It's been ages. How is Kathy doing? You two must have a couple of kids by now."

"No, no kids," he said, "but Kathy and I are fine. What about you? Jeffrey keeps me up on your activities, from time to time. What brings you into our lair?"

I gave him the spiel that Jeffrey and I had rehearsed, and we continued talking, mostly about our careers. I had always known him to be a theater buff and, even though he appeared distracted, he politely questioned me about my role in *Sweeney Todd*. I noticed Tim displayed a nervous habit of rubbing a puffy area just under his right eye, and his face appear strained. This was not at all the same carefree young architect whom I remembered.

After a while, Tim drifted away, and a few other people entered the room. I recognized all three of them from parties I had attended with Jeffrey. It was years ago, and they were all grad students at the time. They appeared to recognize me, and smiled before moving on to the small refrigerator where they helped themselves to drinks.

"Let's get started," Jeffrey said, returning to the head of the table. I sat down next to him. "First off, for those of you who don't know her, I want to introduce Lorelei Waterman Crane, my beautiful ex-wife. Of course, she's better known as the outstanding actress at the Tuscawilla Theater. Lorelei's asked to join us. But I'll let her tell you more. Lor."

Never one to be shy in the spotlight, I stood and described my past work, with the Center, to save development from Paynes Prairie. I then told them about my recent experience in South Florida, and my distress at the overpopulation, overdevelopment, and all the rest. For the sake of authenticity, I salted my spiel with a few f-words, and concluded with a vow to do whatever necessary to stop developers from ruining the State. I sat down hoping I had given a performance convincing enough to get them to trust me. If I read my audience correctly, they bought it.

Jeffrey nodded his approval and resumed the meeting. He reviewed the issues being faced by the environmental community. He gave credit to the Sierra Club for once again helping defeat a change in the comprehensive plan to permit a large development on the rim of the Prairie.

When the St. Johns and Ocklawaha rivers were mentioned, a palpable tension filled the air. Then a young woman, with three eyebrow rings and tattoos covering her upper arms, got up and gave a report on the status of a permit request for a water bottling plant in High Springs. The tension dissipated when she jokingly pointed to the plastic water bottles on the table, and reminded everyone of the old Pogo quote: "We have met the enemy and he is us."

She continued her report by adding, "No kidding. We can't count on the water management district to protect our water supply from bottlers. Look at what happened in Lake County. St. Johns Water Management District approved a new bottling plant even though the county was so water-stressed, its namesake lakes were drying up in the drought. And, by the way, thanks to a bill passed by the Florida Legislature, the water district board no longer holds public hearings. It was the Executive Director who had the sole authority to permit the bottler."

She ended her report by saying, "So, Jeez, you guys, get a stainless steel water bottle, for God's sake. It's embarrassing for us to be supporting the water bottling industry."

From time to time, Jeffrey glanced at his watch. An hour had passed and the meeting seemed to be winding down. Nothing had been said about Adam Kincaid. There had been no opportunity for me to learn anything new or to raise questions about him. I suspected I'd have to meet some of them, one-on-one, in order to learn anything.

As everyone started to leave, Jeffrey asked aloud, "Has anyone heard from Becky?"

The responses were negative.

He gave me a worried look, and whispered, "Becky never misses a meeting. Never."

Chapter 6

I was alarmed by the tone of Jeffrey's question about Becky. I started to ask him about it when we were approached by one of the men who had been sitting in the back of the room.

"I'm worried about Becky," he whispered, taking Jeffrey's arm to pull him aside from the others as they were slowly filing out of the room. I followed the two men.

"If she was going to miss the meeting she would of called. I haven't heard from her since we had a pizza here last night." He paused, and shook his head in a puzzled look. "It's not like Becky. Something must be wrong."

The man was about 5'9", stocky, had black eyes, and smooth dark skin with high cheekbones. His head was shaved except for a rounded top of black hair from which a braid hung down the back of his neck. His voice was deep and husky and had an indiscernible accent.

"It worries me, too," Jeffrey said. "What time did you leave her last night?"

"About eight. She said she was going to stop by a friend's house to feed her cats while she was out of town." He gave me a brief glance, and hesitated before continuing. "I offered to go with her, so we could spend the night together, but she said she'd be going straight home, and needed to get to bed early."

"Hmm," Jeffrey said, rolling his head in an effort to release tension.

"Maybe she decided to spend the night at the friend's house." I suggested. "Do you know her friend's name?"

"No, I think she said Cindy or Kathy. She has so many girlfriends, I didn't really pay attention," he said. "And she wouldn't spend the night there. Becky doesn't like cats—they kill birds."

Jeffrey asked, "Did you try calling her today? At work or on her cell?"

"A couple of times. But I didn't think nothing of it when she didn't call back—at least not till tonight."

Jeffrey took a cell phone out of his shirt pocket and punched in a number. "She's in voice mail."

The man said, "I'm going over to her house to check it out. You wanna come with me?"

Jeffrey nodded and, turning to me said, "Look Lor—oh, I forgot to introduce you. Lorelei this is Bidziil Nelson. We call him Bear."

So this was Becky's boyfriend, I thought, and gave him an appraising look. Becky's taste in men was unpredictable, and I wondered about the attraction to this one.

He acknowledged me with a distracted nod and said, "Let's go. I'm real nervous now."

"I want to come along," I said. "I'm worried, too."

We arrived at Becky's place, in southeast Gainesville, near the Prairie. I rode with Jeffrey, and Bear drove his truck. There were no lights on in the front of the house. Fortunately, Bear had a key to the front door. As we entered, he called out Becky's name and proceeded through the house turning on lights as he went from room to room. Jeffrey followed closely behind him.

I stood at the front entrance and looked around. I hadn't ever been to Becky's house before. It was a modest ranch style house, and the living room had the cluttered look of a collector. Bird photos, Tibetan peace flags, and nature shots hung on the walls, while parts of animal skeletons, seashells, rocks, and books were scattered on every surface, including the floor. The furniture was a thrift shop mix, and there was an aroma of sandalwood incense with a hint of mildew. By all appearances, no one would guess that Becky Haimovitz came from a well-to-do family of Boston professionals.

I continued to hang back as the two men moved about the house and down the hallway to what I guessed to be the bedroom area. Some sense of fear—generated by too many horror and mystery plays—made me reluctant to follow them.

"The bed's unmade, but I can't tell if it's been slept in recently," Jeffrey announced when they returned to the living room.

I felt a wave of relief. Maybe she's spending the night with a friend after all, I thought.

"Check the back porch," Jeffrey suggested to Bear.

We sat on the sofa for what seemed a long time until Bear returned.

He had a dark look on his face when he told us, "There's a hole in the screen, and it's unlocked. The kitchen door lock's broken, too. I put on the outside lights. There's a bunch of footprints in the dirt—all the way out to the woods in back. Don't look good. I don't recall that lock being broke before."

"Shit," Jeffrey exploded, and punched his fist on a coffee table book with enough force that some of the smaller collectibles bounced to the floor. Bear leaned against the doorframe that separated the living room from the kitchen. He looked disheartened.

I began to pick up the things that had fallen to the floor and, looking up at Jeffrey, I said, "Should I call McBride?"

I knew Homer was out of town, but I thought I could call him on his cell phone and he'd give me a contact at the sheriff's office.

"Detective McBride is Lorelei's friend," Jeffrey explained to Bear. "Maybe we should do some checking ourselves before getting the sheriff's office in our business. At least we should try calling a couple of Becky's friends—check out whether she was at work today. You know, we may be making too much of this. After all, her car's gone."

Jeffrey's words were hopeful, but unconvincing. As an actress, I'm an expert in non-verbal behavior—the two men were very concerned. It was clear they believed something bad had happened.

After a few moments of silence, Bear said, "I think someone grabbed Becky."

"Grabbed, as in kidnapped?" I asked, astonished by his assertion. "Why would you think such a thing?"

"Dunno. It just feels that way," he replied, and he started toward the door. "I'm going up to see Carol in Alachua. She'll know if Becky went to work. Maybe she'll know where Becky went to last night."

"Wouldn't it be faster just to call her?" I asked.

Bear turned around at the door, and said, "I don't have her cell phone number. She lives in a trailer on her cousin's property. I've been there before."

Jeffrey thoughtfully rubbed his chin and said, "I'll take Lorelei back to get her car, and check out Lillian's and some of the other downtown pubs. Becky likes to tour the local music scene. She's been known to get wasted and crash with friends."

"Not on the night we have meetings," Bear said and, looking toward the bedroom, added, "and she always makes up her bed in the morning. She told me it's a childhood habit."

"Well, there's a first time for everything," Jeffrey replied. "As for the meeting, maybe she just got tired of listening to the same old crap and wanted to have a good time instead. Believe me the thought's occurred to me more than once." It was Jeffrey trying to convince us of innocent alternatives. Bear and I weren't buying it.

We turned out the lights, Bear locked the house, and we left.

On the way back to Charley's, I told Jeffrey I wanted to go with him to search for Becky.

"You really want to come with me?" he said. "It's getting late, and I know how you like to get to bed early when you're in rehearsals."

"I know, but it'll be better if we both go. While you look around the bars, I can check the ladies' rooms—maybe spot some of Becky's friends. I might be able to find out whose cats she's taking care of."

When Jeffrey dropped me off to get my car at Charley's, I told him I was going to call McBride in the morning. He shrugged and didn't try to talk me out of it. I knew he was now as scared as I was at the thought that Becky was in trouble.

After a restless night, I awoke and looked out the windows to find the day was overcast and gray. It suited my mood. It was well past midnight before I had gotten home. Jeffrey and I found no trace of Becky or her friends at the downtown clubs. Bear called on his way back from Alachua to say that Becky's friend, Carol, had not heard from her. We were all stumped as to her whereabouts. Bear and Jeffrey said they would contact more of Becky's friends today.

I dressed, had some tea and toast and started studying my script in preparation for rehearsals. The thought of Becky kept gnawing at me until I put the script aside and, reluctantly, called Homer. His cell phone was in voice mail. It made me wonder if he would even respond to my call while he was caught up with his son and his wife's divorce action. Just in case I didn't hear back from him, I decided to call Delcie.

"Lorelei? What's gotten you up so early? It's barely nine o'clock. I would've expected you to still be in bed at this hour," she teased.

"Good morning, Del. Well, not so good, actually."

"What's happened?" Her voice was immediately alert and professional.

"Becky's missing."

"Since when?"

I told her about Becky's absence at the Earth Save meeting, what we found when we went to her home, and how we looked for her afterward.

"Were there signs of a struggle at the house?" she asked.

"No, not that we could tell. But the broken locks and footprints…"

"Not conclusive. People live with broken screens and locks— sometimes they've lost their keys and break in themselves. From your description of the house it doesn't seem like she'd be too worried about theft."

"I tried calling Homer, but he's in Atlanta until next week."

"Look, Lorelei," Delcie said. "Given the circumstances. the sheriff's office might not treat this too seriously for a couple of days. She may just be staying at a boyfriend's."

"I think this fellow, Bear, is her boyfriend. And he's very worried."

"Before you get all panicky, maybe you should wait another day to see if she shows up. Now, back up a minute, what were you doing at that Earth Save group?"

"Jeffrey got me to join."

"Good gracious, Lorelei, don't tell me you let him talk you into another caper. That's a really radical group. Remember the last time Jeffrey…"

"Oh, it's not what you think. I actually asked for it. Homer wants me to get inside the group to see if I can find out anything about Adam Kincaid's murder. You know the guy I told you about the other night."

"Hmm, in addition to everything else you're doing, you're now working as a mole for the sheriff's office?"

I ignored her sarcasm.

"So, did you find out anything?"

"No, nothing. Kincaid's name never came up. The meeting was all about the usual environmental issues. Look, Delcie, I really need your help," I said. "I'm convinced something bad's happened to Becky, and Homer's out of town."

Delcie replied in one of her very patient voices. "Like I said, one day AWOL isn't anything to worry about. Maybe she just needed a short vacation from her life. Lord knows, I could use one right about now."

"No, Delcie, don't you remember what I told you?"

"What?"

"About the Kincaid murder, that he was a friend of Becky's, and…"

"Oh yes, of course. Wait a minute, are you thinking this thing with Becky is related to that Kincaid guy?"

"I am. From what Homer told me about his investigation I have cause to worry about both Becky and Jeffrey."

"Tell me what he said, and don't worry about breaking his confidence. I was once a sheriff's deputy, remember?"

I suddenly did feel guilty about not being very good about keeping vows. "I'll just say I'm scared that whoever killed Kincaid may be after his friends, as well. You're the only one I can turn to help find her. Will you help me?"

"Of course, I'll try. Do you know who was the last one to see Becky?"

"I think it was her boyfriend. The Earth Save guy they call Bear. But he's just as puzzled as we are."

"Well, it's a place to start. Can you give me his number, or where I can find him?"

"Jeffrey will know. Call him." I recited Jeffrey's cell phone number which, oddly, I still had memorized.

"Okay, now Lorelei, try not to worry. There's probably a simple explanation for her not showing up. Sometimes people get urges to do things differently, and it throws everyone who depends on them into a panic. Actually, it accounts for a fair portion of my investigation business."

Delcie promised to follow up on the leads I gave her, and to call me as soon as she knew anything.

Shortly after we talked, Homer called.

"What's up, Lorelei? I just got back from breakfast with Bobby. I had my cell off so I just got your message. You sounded stressed."

I related the circumstances of Becky's disappearance to Homer. I apologized for interrupting his visit, and told him that Delcie had agreed to help me. I was hoping he'd offer some suggestions or assistance.

Instead, he replied, "There's not much I can do at this point, and Delcie's a pretty good tracker. I'm sure if Becky's really missing, she'll find her."

His response was disappointing as though he, too, thought I was being an alarmist. I regretted interrupting him at a stressful time of his own, and I asked about his son.

"Oh, he's going to be all right. He doesn't like the idea of us divorcing, but it wasn't like it a big surprise or anything. I'm going to spend a couple of days with him up here—just to make sure he knows I'm always going to be his dad."

"Good idea," I said. "I'm really sorry for dumping all this on you. I just didn't know where else to turn."

"No problem," he said. "By the way, did you find out anything useful from the environmental group?"

"No, but I did make some contacts that might be helpful when I get a chance to meet with them, one on one." I was thinking about

Tim and Bear, as well as the three members of Earth Save who seemed to recognize me from grad parties years ago. "I'll try to get to see at least one of them over the weekend," I said. "In the meantime, what about Becky? In light of what you told me, don't you think her disappearance is too coincidental?" I am nothing if not persistent.

He gave me a pat response. "Let me know if she doesn't show up in a day or so, or if Delcie finds anything suspicious. Otherwise, I'll call you when I get back."

We said goodbye and I checked the time. There was still time before I needed to get to the gym and on to rehearsals. I sat on the sofa and looked out at the lake. The water appeared dull and lifeless under the cloudy sky. The moss on the oak tree branches was billowing in a strong breeze. A rainstorm must be blowing up, I thought. The weather made me want to get back into bed and snuggle under the covers, but I couldn't get Becky off of my mind. Maybe my mental agitation was heightened by the many disappearances caused by the murderous Sweeney Todd.

And what if Bear was right and Becky had been "grabbed," as he said? I'd watched enough TV crime shows to know how important the first twenty-four hours were in finding a kidnap victim. She might need our help and soon.

Chapter 7

Delcie called at five o'clock just as I was leaving the theater on a long break.

"How about meeting for a bite to eat? I'll tell you what I've done about finding Becky and I figured you'd be hungry about now. My treat, but you'll see it on your expense tab." She paused for a reaction, getting none, she added, "Only kidding."

"Dinner? Yes, of course," I said. "I'm actually at loose ends. Where shall we meet?"

"How about the Asian place downtown? It's one of the few restaurants in Gainesville where it's quiet enough to talk."

"Fine," I said. "I'll be there at six."

I stopped by my condo to check the mail and change clothes. I used the directory to get Tim Grantly's phone number. His wife answered.

"Kathy? This is Lorelei Crane. Jeff Waterman's ex. Maybe you don't remember me."

"Of course I do, Lorelei. In fact, Jeffrey still talks about you. He's been such a good friend, and ..." Her voice trailed off as though she had run out of breath.

I said, "Kathy, the reason I'm calling is because I ran into Tim the other day, and there's something I need to talk with him about. When do think he'll be home?"

"I don't know. He hasn't been here all day," she said. "I imagine he's with a client. Tim doesn't always tell me where he's going, or when he'll be back. He likes to be mysterious."

She sounded peevish, as though his secrecy was an issue between them. I hoped she wouldn't ask where I had met Tim. I wouldn't want Tim to think I'd blab.

"Will you leave him a note, or ask him to call me? It's kind of important."

"I can put a note on his desk. Actually, I'm surprised to hear from you. Tim didn't mention you. How long have you been in town?" she asked, in an overly polite way.

"I just arrived a week or so ago."

"Strange you should need to consult my husband, after all these years. I'll let him know you called," she said, coolly, and hung up.

Wow, I thought, crazy lady. I'll have to ask Jeffrey what's going on with her and Tim. Kathy and I hadn't ever been friends. She was always somewhat aloof and, now that I think about it, maybe a little jealous. It was Jeffrey, Tim, and I who would drink into the early morning hours arguing about politics, drugs, and movies. I wondered if she would even tell Tim that I called.

Delcie was seated at a table, in the back of the restaurant, staring out of the window. She was sipping a bright red martini.

"Hi, there," I said, "What're you drinking? It looks delicious."

She looked up, and smiled, "It's pomegranate, you know—real healthy. And don't you love these very cool martini glasses with their artsy stems? I'm going to have to buy some of these." She held hers up to closer inspection.

Delcie always had expensive tastes, and her credit card debt, which she frequently bemoaned, was proof.

The waiter arrived as I sat down and asked for my drink order. "The same," I said, pointing to Delcie's drink.

"So, how was rehearsal?" she asked with genuine interest.

"Have you ever seen the play, or the movie, *Sweeney Todd*?"

"I've seen the previews of the movie with Johnny Depp. Looked too dark and gruesome for my tastes. Tell me about your play. Anybody interesting in the cast?"

During college, Delcie aspired to becoming an actress. Soon after graduation, her experiences led her to believe being an African American was too big a handicap. Yet she never lost her interest in backstage gossip. I told her about some of the cast members, and described the usual gaffs which occur during first rehearsals. I concluded by saying how well I was hitting it off with my co-star, Jeremy Hastings.

The waiter returned with my martini, and Delcie asked, "Is this Hastings your romantic lead?"

"Romantic? You saw the movie previews. My character thinks he's quite ducky—and he uses her—but he could only be called my romantic lead if you think someone who slits people's throats in a barber's chair is your definition of a hot lover."

"Oh, c'mon, Lorelei. You know what I meant. What's the Hastings guy's story? Is he available?"

"I really don't know. We haven't even gotten a chance to talk. But I must say he's given me some interested glances, and he is attractive."

"Oh, good, then there's hope you'll dump Homer McBride for a guy who's more in your league."

"Oh, Delcie, stop being so hard on Homer. He's a good man with too much stress in his life. You know his wife is divorcing him. That's why he's in Atlanta."

"Not surprised," she said, with a dismissive gesture. She motioned to the waiter. "Let's order. The place is starting to fill up."

The waiter came back with my drink, and took our order. I asked for the curried tofu, which Delcie recommended, and she ordered crispy lime tilapia. We agreed to share.

When the waiter left, I broached my main concern. "So, what have you found out about Becky?"

Delcie studied her now empty martini glass for a moment before responding. "Not enough to keep you from worrying," she said. "I talked to the boyfriend. He confirmed that Becky left Charlie's around eight p.m., after they'd had dinner. He walked her to her car, and said she was headed to a girlfriend's house to feed the cats. That's basically all he knows."

"But were you able to find out the girl's name and where she lives?"

"He didn't know, but he gave me the names and numbers of a couple of Becky's friends. I was only able to reach one of them. She gave me some other names. I've been on the phone most of the afternoon networking my way through them, but so far no leads.

None of them knew which friend of Becky's was out of town, and they all seem to have cats."

"Oh, that's discouraging," I said.

"Well, I still have a call out for the other girl Bear mentioned. Maybe we'll get lucky, and she'll know something."

"If she doesn't, I'm going to call Homer again and insist the sheriff's office help find her. He owes me."

Delcie grinned at my self-righteous pique. "That's the spirit. Now, pass over that tofu. I've wanted to try it, but haven't had the courage to order it. Tofu always looks so dammed bland and white, but I do love curry."

We finished our meal and just as the check arrived, Delcie's cell phone sounded. She quickly looked to see who was calling, flipped it open, and responded.

"Hello, this is Delcie Wright. Is this Becky's friend?"

"Yes," the voice said. Delcie had her on a low level of speakerphone.

The dining room was now abuzz with conversation, and I leaned across the table to listen in.

The woman said, "I just got home from work and checked my messages. Sorry I didn't call back earlier, but I have to leave my cell off at work."

"No problem," Delcie said. "We're trying to track down your friend, Becky. She was supposed to be cat-sitting for someone."

"Yeah, she's taking care of Candace Royalton's cats. She's got five of them. What about it?"

"Well, no one's seen Becky since night before last, and we're a little worried about her. Can you tell me where Candace lives?"

"Just a minute, I'll check the exact address. It's kind of hard to find the place. It's tucked into one of those wooded areas along Hogtown Creek."

Delcie took out a pen, her small black Moleskine notebook, placed her cell phone on the table, and waited for the woman to find the address.

"Okay, here it is." She recited the address and phone number.

"Great," Delcie said. "Thanks a lot."

"You don't think anything's happened to Becky, do you?" the woman asked, in a concerned voice.

"Oh, she's probably okay. I'm sure we'll find out she's just been busy showing houses to clients, or something like that. Thanks again for your help."

"Sure, but please call me again if there's anything I can do. I work in the plant lab at the university. You can call me there."

"Ask her if she works with Jeffrey Waterman," I whispered to Delcie.

"By the way, do you work with Jeffrey Waterman?"

"Why yes, how did you know? I'm his lab assistant."

I motioned to Delcie to give me the phone, and said, "Are you Torie Marcus?"

"Yes."

"Hi, Torie. This is Lorelei Crane. I'm a friend of Jeffrey's and Becky's. You're one of the students, who found Adam Kincaid's body, aren't you?"

"Yes," she replied, hesitantly. I heard an intake of breath. "Oh my god, you don't think Becky's in danger because of him, do you?"

"No," I said, trying to be reassuring. "But we might like to talk with you about it at some point. In the meantime, don't worry. We'll find Becky. Thanks for your help. Take care."

I closed the phone and handed it back to Delcie. She had a knowing look on her face.

"I can tell what you're thinking, Lor. You're not that good an actress to fool me."

"Okay, Ms.Private Detective, what am I thinking?"

"You're freaked now that even Torie mentioned a possible connection between Becky's disappearance and the Kincaid murder."

"Well, aren't you?"

Delcie gave a noncommittal shrug, and looked out the window. "Let's get out of here and check the cat lady's house. I think I know where it is. The damn rain's let up a bit, and it's still light enough for us to poke around."

"Okay," I said, checking my watch. "But I have to be back to the theater in an hour. Rick will kill me if I'm late."

Delcie nodded, motioned the waiter to collect our money for the check, and we left.

We took Delcie's SUV, and drove north on 13th Street beyond 39th Avenue. We turned west into an old neighborhood, with large parcels of wooded land, and onto a driveway hidden by a dense canopy of trees.

As she drove on the narrow sandy road, she said, "I've been here before. When I was with the sheriff's office. A couple lived in the cottage at the back of the property. It was a domestic call. The wife was threatening to kill her husband with a kitchen knife. He hid in the bedroom and called 911. Fortunately, we got there in time to calm them both down."

"What set them off?" I asked. My role in *Sweeney Todd* had made me more curious about people's motivation for violence.

"You'll never believe it. Or, maybe you will. He criticized her meat loaf. She threw the pan at him. He threw a bowl of potatoes back at her, and they had a regular food fight—until she went for the kitchen knife. Then he wisely backed off."

"Good lord, it doesn't take much to incite people, does it?"

"Oh, no, I've seen it all," Delcie said. "People can be more vicious than any wild animal—we know how to hurt one another in lot of ways."

The road had potholes, and we bounced up and down as we twisted our way through stands of shrubs and tall trees. After a few minutes, we came to a clearing. I spotted a car parked on the grass in front of a cottage.

"That looks like Becky's new Prius," I said, and felt a wave of relief. "Thank goodness, we've found her." My excitement quickly died when I saw the driver's side door wide open—exposed to the light rain and darkening sky.

Delcie pulled up next to the car, she took a flashlight out of her glove compartment, and we both got out. Delcie immediately started examining Becky's car, and the area around it. "You check out the house," she directed. Motion lights, at the eaves of the roof, came on, and illuminated the front yard.

I went to the cottage, opened the door to the screened in porch, and called out, "Becky are you here?"

There was no answer. I looked through the large porch window and saw that the house was dark. The strong odor of cat urine drew my attention to the two litter boxes on the side of the porch. I could tell they had not been emptied in a couple of days. The cats were nowhere to be seen, but there was a cat door inset into the front door which gave them access to the porch.

"Dammit," I said. "Where the hell are you Becky?" I banged on the front door and tried to open it, but it was locked. There was no one in there. Just the five cats, Torie had mentioned. I hoped they had enough food and water.

"Lorelei, over here," Delcie called. I quickly left the cottage and found her standing at the edge of the mulched driveway. She pointed the flashlight into an overgrown grassy area.

"Look, there seems to be a trail of stuff." She shone the strong light into the wet grass. "I see a lipstick, and over there's a small change purse and some hair clips." She led me through higher grass toward the wooded area south of the cottage. We were both getting soaked as the rain got heavier, but it didn't matter. We were focused on the puzzling scene.

Sensing Delcie's thoughts about the origin of the scattered items, I said, "Over there, that's Becky's handbag. She had it the other day at lunch."

Delcie replied, "It looks like the bag was flung away and the contents scattered all over the place." We stood there for a few moments as Delcie shone her light around the area.

Finally, she said, "C'mon, I don't think it's a good idea to keep looking around out here. The rain's getting worse."

We started back to the house, and she asked, "Did you try to get in there?"

"I did, but the door's locked, and it's dark inside. We might be able to pry open the window. It doesn't look too secure."

"Let's do it," she said. "I hate to mess with a potential crime scene, but if Becky's inside…"

Crime scene? I shivered at the thought as we entered the porch.

Delcie shone her flashlight on the window and on the door, assessing a point of entry.

"You're wearing sturdier shoes than mine," she said. "Kick open the door."

It took surprisingly little effort for the door to give way. Delcie entered first. The overwhelming smell of cat urine made me gag. Several of the cats skittered away from us as we searched the small house. When we entered the kitchen, I switched on the light, and checked to make sure there was enough food and water in their bowls.

"Nobody here except them," Delcie concluded. When we left, she took a tissue out of her pocket and used it on the knob to close the door.

"Now we call the police," she said.

"We got back into her SUV, and she called 911. She identified herself, and told the dispatcher they needed to send a car out to investigate a possible kidnapping."

I listened to her description in alarm.

"You really think she's been kidnapped?" I asked, recalling Bear had made the same assessment.

"Don't know, but it'll get their attention."

"The cats," I said, as we pulled out of the driveway.

"What about them?"

"Give me your cell. I'm going to call Torie, and ask her to take care of them until Candace returns."

Torie agreed to look in on the cats. Delcie drove me back to get my car, and I raced to the theater feeling numbed by the whole incident and its implications.

Chapter 8

"How are you feeling?" the soft voice asked.

As Becky slowly opened her eyes, she first became aware of a pleasant light floral scent coming from the woman squatting next to her.

"Where am I?" Becky turned her head and glanced around. She felt the air mattress underneath her, and saw she was in a large tent. She slowly leaned up on her elbows, and anxiously peered into the woman's face.

"You're in my tent," the woman replied. "We found you at the edge of the creek, and brought you here. You've been asleep for quite awhile. That's good," the woman said, and lightly placed a hand on Becky's forehead, testing for a fever.

"The creek? What was I doing there?" Becky asked, and suddenly feeling dizzy, she collapsed back down, and lifted her hands to her head. "My head's killing me. What happened? How'd I get here?"

"All in due time," the woman said, placing a reassuring hand on Becky's arm. "You've slept for several hours, but you still need more rest. When we found you, it looked like you'd been in the creek all night. But don't worry. You're going to be just fine. We're taking care of you."

Her voice was deep and soothing. Becky looked at her more closely. She was an older woman whose skin held care-worn lines. Her long brown hair, tinged with gray streaks, hung naturally around her face. It was not only her voice, but the woman's eyes that Becky found comforting. They were pale blue and, smiling down at Becky, held a mixture of curiosity and sympathy.

Next, the woman reached beside her, into a shallow bowl, and brought out a compress, which she placed on Becky's forehead. "This should help make your head stop hurting. You had a nasty cut, but I cleaned it out and put a comfrey poultice on it. It's already looking a little better than it did this morning. I didn't think you'd need any stitches; it should heal by itself."

"Thank you," Becky said, feeling relief from the cool towel. "What day is it? Have I been here long?" she asked, and looked down at the flowered gown she was wearing. She felt further confused by the sight of the strange attire.

"It's Saturday," the woman responded, and noticing Becky's reaction to the gown, she added, "You were soaking wet when we found you, so I helped you change into one of my caftans. Now, really, you need to rest. We'll talk later and try to figure out what happened. Just close your eyes and relax. You've apparently had a very bad time, but you're safe now." She patted Becky's arm and moved away.

"Safe," Becky repeated. She felt comforted by the word, and she closed her eyes. As soon as the woman moved from her side, Becky became aware of the tent's aroma—both musty and woodsy. She struggled against her overwhelming weariness, and tried to recall what she was doing in the creek and how she had arrived at this woman's tent. She pictured—in an almost dreamlike recollection— being half lifted from the wet sandy bank, and leaning on the woman as they walked through woods. And, yes, there was a dog. She remembered that. The dog kept dancing around and in front of her like it was leading the way. After that, she must have blacked out, because she couldn't remember getting into the tent, changing clothes, or anything else until now. As she attempted to review the scene again, she started shivering, felt a blanket being laid over her, and she drifted off into a restless sleep.

Becky awoke to the aroma of savory herbs, and realized she was hungry. She looked out of the tent opening. There was a hibachi grill with a pot on top of it. She was also aware of a man's voice outside the tent. She thought it must be the other person who was with the woman.

The woman poked her head into the tent, and said, "Good, you're awake again. We've got to hunker down. Last night's rain was the beginning of a tropical depression. I just heard on the radio that we're going to get a lot of wind and rain for the next couple of days."

Becky rolled on her side and grunted as she tried to push herself up. Her whole body felt stiff and bruised, and she only managed to sit up on the air mattress where she rested before pushing herself farther.

The woman was busy with something on the other side of the tent. When she heard the sounds of Becky's distress, she turned and asked, "Are you hungry?"

"Oh, yes, I am," she said, with a feeling of emptiness in her stomach.

"I made a pot of vegetable soup with some herbs that will help you heal."

The woman left the tent, and Becky watched her as she stooped in front of the hibachi and ladled the steaming liquid into a large ceramic mug. She came back inside and passed the mug to Becky. "Careful, it's hot. Eat it slowly. You probably haven't eaten anything in a day or so."

Becky took the mug, and began sipping the odd tasting liquid. As she did, she surveyed the large tent. It appeared cozy with squares of bright patterned fabric tacked to the tent sides. There were two wicker baskets, which seemed to contain personal items, and a long blue caftan hung near the door. The twin air mattresses were situated along the walls opposite the tent opening. Several colorful cushions, on floor mats, were positioned around a stubby-legged table in the middle of the tent. A florescent lantern hung from the ceiling which was high enough in the center to allow standing.

The woman made up a mug of soup for herself and sat on a cushion, in lotus position, facing Becky.

"My name is Minerva," she said. "What's your name?"

Becky tried hard to think of an answer. She verged on tears, and replied, "I can't think of my name, or how I got here." Her head was throbbing at the effort.

Minerva reached over and patted Becky's leg. "Don't worry, dear. You've obviously been traumatized by your experience. Your memory will come back in a little while."

"Traumatized?" Becky replied, suddenly feeling frightened. "Was I badly injured?" She put down the mug of soup, lifted the caftan, and began to examine the cuts and insect bites on her feet and legs. Her arms, too, were scratched and red with bites."

"When you finish your soup, you can put some more aloe on those bites. I think it's already helped some. You're lucky you didn't get snake bit while you were in the creek. In fact, you might have suffered a bad concussion from the size of the wound on your head. If you were unconscious, it's a good thing you woke up at all."

The severity of her head wound made Becky feel like crying, but she didn't want to upset this woman who was being so kind to her. She stifled her tears, and continued to sip her soup until she could no longer contain her emotions, and blurted, "What do I do now? I can't remember anything about myself."

It was the plea of a lost child, and resonated deeply with Minerva. "Don't worry, dear. Everything is going to be all right. For the present, you are exactly where you should be—right here—and all your needs are being met."

The woman's simple logic and obvious sympathy had a calming effect on Becky.

Minerva continued, "There's a storm coming, but we're pretty secure. This is a good tent. I used the last of my savings to make sure of that. We have enough food and water. Of course, I hope you won't mind sleeping with Fritz. He's the one who really found you and, of course, he'll be in the tent with us."

"Fritz?" Becky asked, wondering if this was the man's voice she had heard before Minerva came into the tent.

"Fritz is my dog companion," Minerva said. "He's very sweet and streetwise, or should I say woods-wise?" She smiled at her own joke. "I share my tent with him at night."

"Oh, the dog," Becky said. "I remember the dog when you helped me out of the creek. He was dancing all around me."

"Yes, I think he's part Australian shepherd. Anyway, Fritz goes into the creek sometimes, and this morning he led me to you."

"Fritz. What a sweet name. How did you name him?" Becky asked. She was beginning to feel better. Maybe it was the soup or the woman's reassurances that made her feel calmer.

"I'm glad you asked. Not many people ask how their dogs get named. I'll tell you. In my younger days, I met a man named Fritz Perls. Have you ever heard of him?"

Becky shook her head.

"No? I guess he would be before your time. Anyway, he was a famous psychotherapist. I had the good fortune to attend one of his workshops in California—in Big Sur. A glorious place. Have you been there?"

"Big Sur?" Becky struggled to recognize the name, and finally said, "I don't know."

Minerva's face took on a meditative look. "I was in my twenties, and it was the experience of a lifetime. Since I've become…well, since I started living as I do now, I often think about that workshop and his ideas. In fact, I've had many conversations with Fritz about my life."

"Conversations? With the dog, Fritz?"

"Oh, yes, my Fritz is a great listener. It really helps to talk about your problems, don't you think? Anyway, Perls approach to therapy was all about awareness, acceptance, and being present. So, when Fritz—the dog—decided to live with me, I named him in honor of my early mentor."

Becky wanted to know more about Minerva, but before she could ask, the woman stood up, and said," Now, if you're feeling up to it, I'd appreciate your help moving a few things into the tent. We need to fortify our campsite."

Becky tried once more to get up, and this time succeeded in standing. Her head and body still hurt, but she instinctively knew it would be better to move around.

The two women left the tent and looked up at the sky. Dark clouds were swiftly moving from the southwest and the wind began to gust. The tops of the tall pines, surrounding the tent, were swaying in the wind. The air smelled damp as it does before a rain. Fritz was roving around the area as though patrolling the perimeter of a fortification. Minerva started to secure the tarp which, held up by poles, created a covering over and at the opening of the tent.

"I just hope this thing doesn't turn into a sail," she said.

At Minerva's direction, Becky brought items in from outside along with clothing, which Minerva said was Becky's, that had dried on a short clothesline attached between two pine trees. In several trips, she collected a green plastic patio table, which held a portable radio and a small statue of Buddha, two folding chairs, several pots of herbs, gardening tools, a short handled broom, and a couple of buckets partially filled with dirt. Minerva told Becky the buckets would serve as latrines if the storm prevented them from going out. Finally, Minerva came into the tent with a bicycle. She placed a large orange water cooler and the hibachi grill next to the tent opening.

Becky sat on the air mattress, feeling exhausted, and watched as Minerva surveyed the crowded tent. At length, she gave Becky a look of satisfaction and said, "That's it then. We have everything we need. It's actually quite snug, don't you think?" She bent out of the tent opening and whistled for Fritz to come in.

At first, the rain came down in large drops pelting the tarp like golf balls, and then the wind began driving it in sheets. Minerva closed the tent flap, and the once seemingly spacious tent felt congested with the three of them, and all of the things brought in from outside. Becky became anxious wondering how she was going to manage being cooped up during the storm. Her anxiety verged on fright, and she struggled to stay calm. She guessed it was late afternoon although the dark clouds had made it seem later. Now, with the tent more or less sealed, it was even darker. She found herself gulping deep breaths to get enough air.

Fritz snuggled next to Minerva who was tuning the radio for a weather report.

"Are you okay?" Minerva asked, turning to see Becky's distress. "I'll make some chamomile tea in a few minutes. It will help to keep us calm. In the meantime, why don't you sit on a cushion over there?" She motioned to a vacant space next to the herb pots.

Becky did as she suggested and, after she moved and inhaled the plants fragrances, she became more relaxed. "I am kind of nervous about the storm," she said to Minerva. "Maybe we should have found a shelter or something."

"No, we'll be fine. Fritz and I have ridden out storms before. Don't worry. I want to save the lantern for nighttime, but I'll light a candle so we can at least see one another better."

Minerva lit a candle and placed it on the table next to the small Buddha statue. She continued tuning the radio, until she found a clear signal, and listened intently to the weather forecast. The storm was in progress.

Becky stared at the statue of the seated smiling Buddha and hoped it would protect them somehow. The candle cast an eerie glow, but did make her feel a little less claustrophobic. She shifted her gaze, to the woman and her dog, and listened to the thunder growing louder and closer as it announced the strengthening storm. The scene in the tent took on a dreamlike quality. She pinched herself hoping it was a dream and that she would awaken...but where?

Minerva lit a canister of fuel in the hibachi grill and put a small pan of water on to heat. "We'll have some tea. It will make you feel better. And we can talk. Good conversation is a great distraction during a storm. Maybe you'll even remember enough to tell me about yourself."

Becky moved her head from side to side, in a gesture of defeat, and took a deep breath. "I'd be glad to talk, but I really can't think what to say. Maybe it would be better if you told me about yourself. What are you doing living in a tent alone in the woods?"

The woman let out a strange broken laugh, and said, "Alone? I'm not alone. I've got Fritz here, and now you've arrived. Don't you see? Everything's perfect."

Perfectly crazy, Becky thought, and shivered at the damp chill that had entered the tent. She continued to study Minerva as the woman prepared their tea. Even in the dim candlelight, Becky noticed how disheveled she looked. She anxiously began to wonder if Minerva was the kind of mental case like some of those homeless women she'd seen... somewhere.

Finally, Minerva passed a mug of tea to Becky, and said, "Here, dear, drink this. It will make you feel relaxed. You're going to be just fine. You'll see."

Chapter 9

The ringing in my ears was not my alarm clock, it was the phone. I rolled over on the bed and grabbed the receiver.

"Hello," I mumbled, still groggy from a deep sleep.

"Lorelei, it's Jeffrey."

I pushed up my sleep mask and looked at the bedside digital clock. It was 7:34 a.m. "Jeffrey? Why in the world are you calling so early? I feel like I just fell asleep."

"Sorry Red, I've been having trouble sleeping myself. The thing is, I'm heading off on a field trip with a group of students."

I sat up on the side of the bed and tried to gather my wits. I had taken a sleeping pill at two in the morning, after tossing and turning for hours, and was having trouble clearing my head.

"Oh, God, of course," I said. "You're returning my call from last night."

"Yes, I was into something and had my cell phone on silent."

Into something, or someone? I wondered.

He continued, "By the time I got your message I thought you'd be asleep. What in the hell happened to Becky? You said you and Delcie found her car?"

I took a deep breath and looked out the windows. It was dark, gusty, and pouring rain.

"You're going on a field trip in this weather?" I asked.

"It's an indoor plant show in St. Augustine. But never mind, tell me about Becky."

By now, I felt slightly more awake, and walked over to look out of the window. "It's pretty much like I said in my message. Delcie and I found where Becky was to be cat-sitting. Your lab assistant, Torie, gave us the address."

"Yes, she told me you called her. So you went there and what?"

"We found Becky's car. The driver's door was open like she had gotten out in a real hurry. Delcie spotted a lot of stuff scattered on the ground, like it'd been thrown from a purse, and Becky's handbag. Then, we broke in and searched the cottage. There was nobody there, but the cats. It looked—no smelled—like their litter hadn't been changed in a couple of days."

"Jeez, and no other sign of Becky?"

"Nope. Delcie called the police. I had to get back to the theater, so we left before they arrived."

"That doesn't sound good."

"No, it doesn't, Jeffrey. Delcie went back there after she dropped me at my car. I went on to rehearsals, but I was so upset. I had trouble even remembering my lines."

"I guess so. What did the cops find? Do you know?"

"I talked to Delcie later during a break, and she said they didn't find Becky. The officers looked around, and walked down to the creek but, in the heavy rain, it was impossible to see anything that might be a clue."

I heard Jeffrey sigh on the other end of the phone. "I don't know what to say. I tried calling Becky's cell phone all day and got no response. Bear's been out looking, too. It's Saturday, and she's been missing, so far as we know, since our meeting."

"Well, thanks to Delcie, at least the police are involved now. I'll be in rehearsals all day and evening. We're on a weekend marathon because of the students' schedules. But I'll call you on my dinner break if Delcie's found out anything new."

"Okay, I'll appreciate it, Lor. God, if anything's happened to Becky…" Before his voice trailed off, I'd heard the catch in his voice.

"Don't worry, Jeffrey," I said, trying to provide reassurance I didn't feel, "You know what tough character she is."

"Yeah," he replied, solemnly, "So was Stoker."

I shivered at the thought that he linked the two events. "Jeffrey, don't you think we should call Becky's parents? You have their number in Boston, don't you?"

He groaned. "Do you really think we should worry them yet?"

"Yes, I do. Just in case, you know."

"Maybe you're right. I'll try to get away from the kids, when we get to St. Augustine, and call them. But what in the world should I tell them?" He hesitated before saying, "You're so much better at it, Lor, how about it if I give you their number and you call them?"

"The hell I will, Jeffrey Waterman." I felt indignant that he tried to put it off on me. After all, he had lived with Becky and, for a time, they had an intimate relationship. If anything, Becky was more his responsibility than mine.

"Okay, take it easy. No harm asking. I'll tell them she's missing, but…"

"Just try telling them the truth, Jeffrey—they're her parents— they have a right to know everything we know. Tell them all of her friends are looking for her, and suggest that they call the Gainesville Police Department."

"You're right. They need to know."

"Let's try to stay as positive as we can. Remember, no news is good news. I'll talk to you later. And, Jeffrey," I paused, looking out at the storm, as my mind flashed to an earlier scene in which Jeffrey and I had a terrible car accident on the same road to St. Augustine. "Please drive carefully. It's nasty out there."

I did my yoga routine, dressed, and had breakfast. Afterward, I got ready to study for rehearsals. I set up my reference books, and the *Sweeney Todd* script at the dining room table. It was almost nine thirty when Delcie called.

She said, "I spoke with one of my buddies at the police department. He told me they still haven't found evidence of foul play. He said the open car door was unusual, but not conclusive. And, by the way, they weren't impressed by the scattered cosmetics as evidence of anything."

"So Becky's just vanished?"

"It appears that way, Lorelei."

"Well, we know better. Something or someone caused her to leave her car in such a panic. Can they at least report Becky as a missing person? It's been more than 24 hours since she was seen. Isn't that enough time?"

She laughed, "There's no wait time to report a missing person in Alachua County. That's a popular misconception. Do you want to make the report?"

"I spoke to Jeffrey and asked him to call Becky's parents, in Boston. They should probably make the report, but I don't think we ought to wait. Can you do it, Del? Jeffrey's going to be in St. Augustine, and I'll be in rehearsals until God knows what time tonight."

"Okay, I'll see if I can pull it off. If I don't have enough information, I'll call Bear. He was the last one to see her anyway."

When I got off the phone with Delcie, I tried calling Tim Grantly at his home again. I wished I had remembered to ask Jeffrey for Tim's cell phone number. Kathy answered the phone.

"He's out of town, Lorelei. And, I don't know when he'll be back."

"You didn't tell me he was leaving town when I spoke with you yesterday," I said, with a spark of annoyance. Listening to the pitch of my voice, I realized how stressed I was.

"Well don't blame me," she said. "I didn't know he was going until he called me last night from someplace in Colorado. He didn't even pack any clothes. Claimed it was an emergency visit to a client, and he'd pick up some clothing while he was there. He was real vague and stressed-out on the phone. I don't know what's got into him lately. As if our marriage wasn't already in trouble, he goes and disappears on me. But I'm worried about him."

I felt a sudden rush of sympathy for Kathy. "Sorry I was so irritable, Kathy. I'm under a lot of pressure right now, and I would really like to talk with Tim. Can you give me his cell phone number?"

"All right, but don't count on his answering. He says he sometimes forgets to charge it. I think he just turns the thing off when he doesn't want to talk to me. If I didn't know him so well I'd think he was having an affair, or something." She ended with a false laugh.

"I'll take a chance on calling him. What's the number?" I wrote down the number she recited. I knew I had to learn more about Stoker's death, and it might give me a clue about Becky. I hoped Tim would provide me with some answers.

When I called his cell phone, I got a message that the caller was out of his calling zone. "Shit," I said. "Just where in hell have you disappeared to, Grantly?"

I made a second cup of green tea, and returned to the dining room table. I thought, you've got to focus, Lorelei. You can't mess up another rehearsal. Renee anointed you the doyenne—you've got to set a better example.

I needed some background research for my role as Mrs. Lovett. I scanned copies of the original script, and the Sondheim/Wheeler book—subtitled *A Musical Thriller*. I looked for anything that would inform the character of Mrs. Lovett. Robert Mack's scholarly work contained the Todd story. The nineteenth century original first appeared as an English serial, *The String of Pearls: A Romance*, snd was the one adapted for the theater. The stories had numerous spinoffs in publications known as "penny bloods" or "penny dreadfuls." It was a genre that aptly described the melodramatic and shocking tales.

Mrs. Lovett, Todd's sometimes business partner; sometimes lover has various names such as Nellie, Marjorie, Sarah, and others. In some versions, she assisted Todd—and her own failing pie business—by cutting up the bodies and making them into veal meat pies. Mack observed that cannibalistic tales weren't new—they dated as far back as Homer's *Odyssey*—and were found in fairy and folk tales throughout the ages. In 1847, the writer was likely influenced by a contemporary Charles Dickens novel, *Martin Chuzzlewit*, where a character says that visitors to London might wind up being "made meat pies of or some horrible thing."

I was surprised to learn about the enduring popularity of the Sweeney Todd story. Since it's original appearance, it has not only been a theater staple in England, but has been adapted as an opera, a concert work, popular comic song, graphic novel, young persons novel, radio show, ballet, three early English musicals—before Sondheim's Broadway show—three early twentieth-century movies, a BBC production and two recent movies: John Schlesinger's *The Tale of Sweeney Todd* (1998) and Tim Burton's *Sweeney Todd: The Demon of Fleet Street* (2007). Quite a run, I thought.

77

I reflected on the reaction of my fellow actors to the play, and decided they were all correct in their assessment of the characters. Todd and Mrs. Lovett shared traits of cunning and greed. Todd plays on Mrs. Lovett's affections to achieve his revenge. She, in turn, sees their partnership as a shrewd business opportunity. Foolishly, she falls in love, plans to marry him and retire to the seaside. They both behave like psychopaths—charming, but callous. In the end, Todd learns Lovett lied to him about his wife's death, and he shoves her into one of her own ovens. An ironic finale for the love struck pie maker.

I relished the story, and was working on memorizing my lines when the cell phone went off. I didn't recognize the number on the ID screen.

"Lorelei, this is Tim. Kathy said you needed to talk to me."

"Tim, I'm glad you called back."

So intensely had I been into my homework, that it took me a moment to recall what it was I wanted from him.

"I can't talk long, but Kathy said your call sounded urgent."

"Yes, it is," I said, getting my head back into Becky's disappearance. "It's about Becky. She's been missing for several days. We're afraid something bad has happened to her."

There was a long pause before he responded, "I'm sorry to hear that, but what can I do? I don't know when I'll be back in Gainesville."

"I thought you might know something about Adam Kincaid's death. Maybe something you failed to tell the police—that might explain Becky's…"

"Why do you think I know about Stoker's murder?" He said in a tight voice, "Listen Lorelei, take my advice. Let the police deal with Becky's disappearance. It's too dangerous. You need to stop asking questions."

"Dangerous? How? Is there some connection?" I suddenly thought my worst fears were about to be realized.

"There's nothing more I have to say," he said. "And, please, don't try calling me or Kathy again. She's upset enough as it is."

"Are you in trouble, Tim? You sound really stressed."

There was another long pause before he spoke, "Ask Jeffrey about Rodman Dam."

He abruptly ended the call. When I tried to redial there was no dial tone. I checked my received calls, and the number for Tim's call didn't match up with the number Kathy had given me. What the hell is going on with you, Tim? You've not only left town in a big hurry, your wife doesn't know where you are, you warn me not to try and talk with either one of you, and now you're using another cell phone. How does it all relate to what Jeffrey could tell me about the Rodman Dam? Rather than getting any answers from Tim, I now felt completely mystified.

Chapter 10

Tim's responses only heightened my fears about Becky's safety. His obvious paranoia intensified my suspicion of a connection between Becky's disappearance and Adam Kincaid's death. I was eager to learn Jeffrey's reaction to Tim's comment about the Rodman. But I'd have to be disciplined, and get back to my real work. Rehearsals were scheduled to go on well into the evening.

They did and I came home exhausted. It was early Sunday morning when Jeffrey called.

"Hi, Red. Hope I didn't wake you again."

"No, I've been up for an hour or so. I'm glad you called. Did you get in touch with Becky's parents?"

"Yes, and it wasn't fun, believe me. Anyway, they're coming down. I got them a room at the Holiday Inn."

"Good, you did the right thing," I said. "Jeffrey, I need to talk with you about Tim Grantly."

"Tim? Okay, I need to go to the Science Library this afternoon, but I was going to ask you to join me for brunch anyway. We could talk then. How about it?"

I quickly calculated the time before rehearsals began, and said, "Yes, that'd be fine. Where do you want to meet?"

"The old Pizza Palace on 13th has really good breakfasts. Can you make it in a half an hour?"

"Yes. In a half hour," I said. I smiled thinking about how Jeffrey's tastes in food had not progressed since college—pizza, hamburgers, and beer were always his staples. Considering his eating habits, I was envious that he continued to look youthful and slim, while I had to do strenuous exercise and undergo periodic diets. Not fair, I thought.

I met him inside the restaurant and we were seated at a small table by the window. It was still raining and windy from the weather system passing through North Florida. The waiter took our order. I looked around at the funky wall murals, and said, "Why do you always want to meet me at places like this?"

"Like what?" he responded, looking surprised.

"Places where you and I have a history. First the Swamp, then Charley's and now here."

He shrugged helplessly, and replied, "Honestly, Red. I didn't even think about it. They're just all close to campus. But now that you mention it, do you remember we ate here on our first date?"

Returning Jeffrey's soft gaze, my mind traveled back to the year I was in the MFA program at the university. I had met Jeffrey during an environmental fight to stop development in Jonesville. His commitment and personal magnetism won me over and—if I were to be honest with myself—stirred me to this day. Of all the feelings I had about Jeffrey Waterman, admiration was at the top of the list.

"Yes, I do. 1988 was an interesting year," I said, "And do you remember what happened right here a few days after our date?"

He thought for a moment. "There was a fire, and the place closed down for a few years. Boy, I really missed it. It was a major student hangout. By the way, did you know, the Original Pizza Palace opened in Gainesville in 1950s—it was the first pizza franchise in the country. How about that for a little bit of Gainesville history?"

"You and your little factoids," I said. "You should be on *Jeopardy*. Look, before our food comes, I want to talk with you about Tim."

"Did you meet with him to do your little mole thing for Detective McBride?"

"No, and I've had nothing but the strangest encounters with both Tim and Kathy."

"What do you mean?"

The food arrived, and I said, "Let's wait until we finish eating. I know how you hate cold food."

When we finished eating, I told Jeffrey about my bizarre conversations with Kathy Grantly. Then, I told him about my call to Tim, and his mysterious comment about the Rodman.

Jeffrey looked completely taken aback by my story. "Rodman? You mean Kirkpatrick Dam. They changed the name, but I can hardly bring myself to call it that. George Kirkpatrick was one of the powerful legislators who succeeded in stopping restoration."

"Whatever," I said. "Why would Tim want me to ask you about it? And why was he so nervous?"

"I really don't know," Jeffrey said, taking a sip of his Pepsi. "When the Rodman spillway was blown up…"

"Blown up?" I felt a shock through my body as though I had touched a live wire. "Blown up?" I repeated, in a high pitched voice loud enough to draw attention from a couple seated nearby.

Jeffrey put a finger to his lips to urge me to lower my voice.

"When did that happen?" I whispered.

"Oh, c'mon, Lorelei. You can't have been so oblivious down there not to know the gates of the dam were breached. It happened about two and half months ago. It was all over the news. It even made national headlines. At first they thought it was done by foreign terrorists."

I quickly calculated what I was doing two and half months ago. It was in April that mother had her second, more serious stroke. I was spending all my time at the hospital, looking for nursing homes, dealing with the realtor for the sale of our house, or at the theater. I think everyone must have a time in their life, like that, when they're wholly wrapped up in their own small world

"I guess I was oblivious. I had a lot going on with my mother's illness and the theater at that time. I wasn't watching TV or reading the newspapers. Tell me what happened."

"Well, you know a lot of people were tired of all the politics keeping the dam from being decommissioned. The legislature gave lip service to having it breeched, but never funded it. Meanwhile, a lot of folks in Putnam County, and elsewhere, who liked bass fishing and duck hunting in the reservoir kept the pressure on to leave it alone. They even got the stinking Rodman reservoir renamed Lake

Ocklawaha. You know the reservoir was designed, for the Cross Florida State Barge Canal, to store water to float the barges. It's nothing but a big fishing hole on top of what was a part of the Ocala National Forest, and some 20 natural springs. Anyway, one of the local groups defending it calls it a wildlife paradise. Hell, any resemblance to the Ocklawaha paradise, before it was dismembered, is a bad joke."

I said, "I remember seeing photos of the reservoir a few years ago. All the dead trees sticking out of the water. It looked like a forest graveyard."

"That's exactly what it was. After a while, the people who wanted to keep the river dammed, built it up as some kind of major recreation area with campsites and all sorts of stuff. The way they tried to make it permanent was by renaming things—like we'd forget that the Kirkpatrick Dam was really the Rodman, and the so-called Lake Ocklawaha was really just a shallow pool of water filled with dead trees, silt and hydrilla. Some loony tunes even proposed putting a huge marina on the shallow end of it."

He shook his head and with a look of disgust, added, "Amazing, isn't it?"

"It is after all the years of work, by environmental organizations, to have it dismantled."

Jeffrey nodded and let out a loud sigh. "It's hard to believe, but it's been about forty years since the dam was built for the Barge Canal—talk about your roads to nowhere. Every Florida governor since Claude Kirk has been in favor of restoration—for all the good it's done. I do have to give credit to Republican presidents though. It was Nixon who suspended work on the canal in 1971 and George Bush, Sr. who deauthorized the project and changed its purpose to recreation and conservation in 1990."

I said, "But at least they gave Barge Canal land for the Marjorie Harris Carr Cross Florida Greenway. As I recall it's a 110 mile green corridor from the St. Johns River to the Gulf of Mexico."

"Sure, it's the only positive thing to come out of it all. Marjorie Carr was quite a woman. She led the fight on the issue practically the last third of her life. It's certainly fitting that her name's on the land.

Hell, if she were still alive, she'd be one happy woman now. Someone finally got tired of waiting and blew the thing up." He laughed. "Lor, you just can't imagine how many people were thrilled by it. There were actually Ocklawaha River celebration parties."

"I would have been there. What happened afterward?" I asked, totally captivated by the event.

He laughed and tapped his straw against the now empty drink glass. The waiter noticed and came by with a refill. Jeffrey took a few sips and continued.

"As you might have expected all hell broke loose. Florida Department of Environmental Protection, FEMA, OGT, the governor and the legislature all got involved trying to decide what to do about it. It was a three ring political circus. Some wanted the Corps of Engineers to patch the spillway with concrete; others said, let it alone. They reasoned since the dam was going to come down someday anyway, why not save the State the millions of dollars in dismantling costs?"

"What'd they decide to do?"

"Before any of the power brokers could persuade the Corps to patch it, word went out to all the environmental groups. Oh, it was a sight to see. I can't believe you didn't read about it. All sorts of people went to the dam and staged a vigil—climbed up on the broken concrete and steel fragments of the gates, and vowed not to allow anyone to patch it, or clear it. I think some of them may still be holding demonstrations there."

"Wow. Was the reservoir completely drained when the dam broke?"

"No. It was a surprise. After the initial surge, tons of concrete, logs and debris kind of blocked the spillway. The water just started to seep through in a nice flow. In fact, if we can keep the pressure on the DEP to stall making a decision—we'll have achieved passable restoration, after all. It's really cool. They say that some of the fish are already coming back into the Ocklawaha and the Silver River. And the manatees, which used to be killed in the locks, can safely return to their former habitat."

"Jeffrey, believe it or not, I've never even been to the river and the dam. I want to go over and see it," I said. "Will you take me?"

"Much as I'd love to, I'm really pressed right now. But you can find it yourself. Look, I'll draw you a map of the area." He reached into his briefcase, pulled out a sheet of paper, a flow pen and started sketching. "You know how to get to Palatka on SR 26. If you want to see the dam, turn south on Highway 19 to the green sign for the Cross Florida Greenway—it's just after you cross the bridge," he said, as he made quick lines on the paper. "I'll just put in some of the other roads and where the St.Johns River fits into the picture."

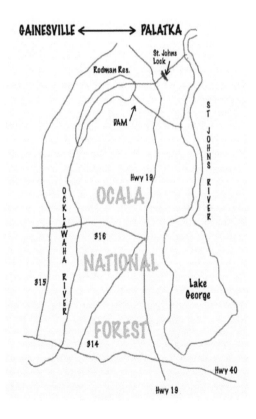

He finished the sketch, looked it over and—with a satisfied smile, he handed it to me.

I said, "What a cool little map, Jeffrey, thank you." I folded it and put it into my handbag.

He said, "Better yet, if you don't want to go alone, call Sharon Adelle with the Sierra Club over there. She's a friend of mine, and she'll fill you in on the local scene. She may even take you out on the river and show you the dam."

"That would be great," I said, and suddenly remembered Tim Grantly. "But why did Tim want me to ask you about Rodman? He couldn't have known I hadn't heard about it."

"I don't know. It sounds like he was stressed-out when you talked to him."

I leaned forward and, in a soft voice, said, "Jeffrey, you can trust me. Did Earth Save have anything to do with it?"

He gave me a quizzical look before saying, "Hell no, Lorelei. I may be impulsive, but I'm not a complete fool." He also lowered his voice, and added, "Sure, I fantasized blowing the thing up. So did lots of other people."

"I'm still trying to figure out why Tim mentioned Rodman when I asked if there was a connection between Becky's disappearance and Stoker's murder."

"I told you, I don't know. For God's sake, soon after the explosion, the FBI, FDLE, and a bunch of other agencies grilled lots of people, including all the Earth Save members. I told them, anyone who knew how to handle explosives could have done it. That includes people in construction, the military, and who knows how many others. It's all on the web now, isn't it?"

"How did they even get to you, or know who the members were? I thought you didn't keep membership lists."

"Are you kidding? They know. Besides, there was the little matter of arrests at the Paynes Prairie rally, and even as far back as Jonesville."

"And Becky, Tim and Stoker were questioned by the FBI?"

"Yes, but they found nothing on any of us."

"So, have they found out who did it?" I asked.

"Hell, no. From time to time, there's a news story about the investigation continuing, and asking people for information. There's even a reward for anyone with information leading to the so-called terrorists. That's what they're calling them. Well, at least in this case, I'd say one man's terrorist is another man's hero."

"Ssssh, Jeffrey, you shouldn't talk like that. Someone might hear you."

"Dammit, Lorelei, last time I heard this is still a free country. I'm allowed to voice my opinion."

"Let's get out of here before you get yourself into trouble. I want to talk about this some more."

He beckoned the waiter for our check, paid it, and we left. I checked the time and knew I was due at the theater in a half an hour. We sat in my car, and I quietly asked Jeffrey, "Okay, I believe you when you tell me you weren't involved in the Rodman sabotage but, tell me the truth, do you think it's possible that other members of Earth Save could have been—without you knowing about it?"

Jeffrey turned, and looked away for what seemed a long time before answering. He had a troubled look on his face.

"I would only tell this to you, and you mustn't ever repeat it. Of course, it is possible."

I thought back to the Earth Save meeting, and the inexplicable tension at the mention of the Ocklawaha River. I said, "Jeffrey, you know Becky may well be in danger if she's not already been harmed. We have to find her as soon as possible. If you think Stoker was involved maybe Becky was, too. Homer can help us find her, but he'd need to know the truth."

Jeffrey angrily slammed his hand on the dashboard. "Are you insane? There's no way in hell I'd allow you to give him any information to implicate our friends in this. You don't seem to understand the severity of it all. Did I mention FBI? Aside from major criminal charges, feelings are still running really high about the breach. Some of the locals there would crucify anyone they thought had anything to do with blowing up the dam."

"Okay then," I said. "I get it. I won't say anything to Homer. I'll ask Delcie to help. We can trust her."

"Lorelei, you can't trust anyone with allegations about this. But, if you must, please, tell her as little as possible."

"Okay, I understand, but you have to tell me if you think Becky was involved. It would explain a lot."

He shrugged, in a weary gesture. "I genuinely don't know. I really doubt it, but if anyone does know, it might be her boyfriend, Bear."

Chapter 11

Monday was our day off from rehearsals. Before I left the condo, I put in a call to Bear, and left a message that I wanted to see him. Afterward, I headed to the gym. I hated working out on my day off, but I knew I needed to stay in shape. Pam's all-terrain cycling class was, as always, an exhilarating but exhausting hour-long workout. Afterward, I spent time in the spa area to relax and loosen up my muscles. I finally left the club about noon.

The rain had finally stopped, and the inside of my car was like a sauna from sitting in the sun for two hours. I got in and left the car door open until the AC started cranking. At the same time, I checked my cell phone. Bear had returned my call. I punched in his number.

"Hi, this is Lorelei. Thanks for calling me back. I've been at the gym."

"No problem. Have you heard anything about Becky?"

"No, I haven't. That's why I called you. Any chance I could see you today? I'm off work, and have the time to meet, if you do."

He hesitated. "Why do you want to see me?" He sounded defensive.

"I thought we could put our heads together to figure out where Becky is," I said, concealing the question I really wanted to ask him.

He said, "I don't know where she is. I call her friend, Carol, every day to see if she's heard from Becky."

"Well, it couldn't hurt to talk about it. At the same time, I can fill you in on what's happened in last couple of days. Please, Bear, will you meet me? We both want to find her, don't we?"

He hesitated again before responding. "Okay. Do you know where the bakery is in High Springs?"

"High Springs? I thought you were in Gainesville."

"Not now. I stay with friends near High Springs. I don't come in to Gainesville."

"But I thought you worked in Gainesville?"

"I'm a computer guy. I work anywhere," he said. "So, do you know the place I mean? It's along the railroad tracks off Main Street."

"Yes, I think I do. Can we meet around three this afternoon?"

"I'll see you then," he said, ending the conversation.

Hmm, I thought, a man of few words. I wondered why he was staying in High Springs, and why he didn't even sound very receptive to brainstorming Becky's whereabouts.

I drove up Highway 441 to High Springs, and found the place he suggested we meet. As I was parking, I noticed Bear standing outside of the building. I waved to him. From a distance, I wouldn't have recognized him if I hadn't seen him before, and expected to see him now. His black hair was covered by a cowboy hat pulled down over his eyes; he had on bib overalls and a long sleeved cowboy shirt. He looked dressed like he was coming into town for the farmers market.

"Hi, do you want to go inside?" I asked when I joined him.

"No, better talk outside," he said. "There's a bench over there." He gestured to a clump of trees a half a block away.

He led me to a wooden bench under a large moss covered oak tree. After we sat down, I told Bear what had happened since I last saw him at Becky's cottage. I described what we had found at the house where Becky was believed to be cat-sitting. I also told him about the missing person's report and Jeffrey's call to Becky's parents. I didn't mention anything about Tim. I still hadn't figured that angle out.

Bear sat hunched over, with his elbows resting on his knees, as he listened to me. When I finished, he nodded and, still not looking at me, said "Yeah, Jeff told me some of the stuff. But I already knew it was bad when we was at her place that night."

"You did? Well, I wasn't so worried until we found her car, you know? And now, I'm not only wondering where she is, but why she disappeared in the first place? Aren't you? I mean, if we knew why she was gone it might help to find her. Do you have any ideas about it?"

"Dunno where, or why," he said.

"Look, Bear. Let me be honest with you. Jeffrey didn't come right out and say so, but I think he suspects a connection between Becky's disappearance and Stoker's murder. I didn't know anything about the Rodman Dam being blown until yesterday." Bear tensed as I continued. "If there's any chance that Stoker and Becky were involved in it," I paused. "Well, it would explain a lot. What do you think?"

"Why do you think Becky was involved?" he asked. I sensed that his body had shifted slightly away from me and, when he sat up, he continued staring at the ground. I also noticed he was perspiring although there was a cool breeze in the shade.

"Please, you can trust me. I'm happy the dam was breached. I only want to find Becky before it's too late. Was she involved or not? You two were very close, you must know something."

He finally looked at me, but I was unable to read his expression.

"So, what do you think about it?" I persisted.

He shrugged, and bent over to pick up a stick from the ground. "What do you expect me to say? The FBI and others already asked us lots of questions about the dam. We all knew some thought Earth Save might of done the bombing, but they couldn't prove anything. If you're so curious, why don't you ask them what they know about who did it?"

"Are you kidding? The FBI wouldn't tell me anything. I'm just a concerned friend."

I knew I had to keep on pushing him, even though I suspected he wasn't going to budge. After a few moments of silence, I said, "I spoke with Tim Grantly a couple of days ago."

"You talked to Tim?" he said, shooting me a wary glance.

"Yes," I said, feeling I had hit upon something. "He's out in Colorado, you know, and he apparently left town in a hurry. Even his wife is puzzled by his behavior. I found it pretty strange, when I asked him about Becky, he mentioned the Rodman Dam. What do you make of that?"

Bear kept his head down, and started drawing quick lines in the dirt with the stick he had picked up. He was clearly getting more agitated.

"Dunno," he stubbornly repeated. He looked at me again, and said, "Look, Lorelei, you're a nice lady. I know you mean well, but I don't think you should go around asking all these questions. You'll just make more trouble."

"Trouble for you? Is that why you and Tim have left Gainesville? Because of Stoker's death and Becky's disappearance?"

He didn't respond.

"You're afraid someone's out to get you. Who do you think it is?"

"Could be some white guys who think we was the one's who messed with their fishing hole."

"Do you mean...?" I stopped in mid-sentence. Was he hinting that they were all in trouble for being suspected of blowing up the dam?

As if reading my mind, he said, "Don't think too much about what I said. It was just a joke. Anyway, I gotta go now." He stood up and added, "I probably shouldn't have said I'd meet you. Won't do Becky no good, but I'd like to know if you find out anything about her."

"I'll let you know, and I'd appreciate it if you'd consider telling me why you think she's disappeared," I said.

He touched the brim of his hat, and walked away.

I sat there wondering about his "just joking" comment. It seemed to me that he and Tim were certainly behaving like they were frightened of being the targets of a revenge plot—rightly or wrongly accused.

As I walked to my car and started to pass the bakery, I noticed they sold ice cream and I couldn't resist the urge. I really needed a break before I began thinking about the meeting with Bear. Something with dark chocolate would be helpful—maybe even a sundae with lots of fudge and whipped cream. Mrs. Lovett definitely needed a break from those vile meat pies.

Later, on my way back to Gainesville, I reviewed the essential elements of my inquiries—murder, possible revenge, and paranoia— all of which applied both to my play and to this real-life investigation. It wasn't the first time I found myself involved plots in which art imitated life, or vice versa. Perhaps it was the reason I so relished being involved in both activities—it was the stuff of classic drama.

"Hi, Lorelei, I'm back." the voice announced when I picked up the phone in my condo.

"Homer? How are you? Did everything go well in Atlanta?" I asked.

"Pretty much what I expected. It's okay. My son will still spend part of his summers with me. In fact, he'll be coming in a week or so. I'd like you to meet him."

"Yes, I'd like that too," I said, trying to imagine a junior version of Homer McBride.

"Anyway," he continued, "how about that dinner I promised you? Are you free tonight? I thought I remembered that Monday's were always your days off."

"That's right. I'd love to have dinner with you. Actually, I have some questions I want to ask you about the Kincaid case."

He groaned. "Questions about a case? What kind of Frankenstein have I created? Can't we just have a friendly dinner without talking about murder?"

An odd response from a homicide detective, I thought. Yet, on the other hand, if I were in his shoes maybe I'd need a break from my daily reality.

"Homer, Becky is still missing, and the situation is more urgent than I originally thought."

"Okay, okay. I don't like to talk about criminal matters in public places. How about if I pick up a pizza and bring up to your condo."

"Great idea," I said. "Mushrooms and extra cheese, in case you were going to ask. I'll provide the wine or beer."

"Seven o'clock okay for you?" he asked.

"Fine," I said, and gave him directions. I was excited at the prospect of being alone with Homer. It would not only give me some time to talk about my questions and fears for Becky but also...what? I wondered, do I really want to move our relationship to another level? "Well, Lorelei," I said aloud, "let's not overthink this thing. Just relax and let happen what feels right at the time."

He arrived a little after seven. I placed the pizza in the oven to stay warming, and served some snacks—pretzels, olives, and celery—along with a glass of Merlot for me and a Sam Adams for him. I settled on the couch and he took the armchair across from me.

"Nice view," he said, and scanning the living area of the condo, he added, "but aren't you a little cramped here? Why'd you give up that beautiful home down in Micanopy?"

"The one with Bill?" I asked, with a touch of sarcasm.

"Yeah, I see. Anyway, let's get over the business part of the evening so we can talk like real people—whatever that's like."

"Where to begin?" I said. "You know about the missing person's report that Delcie arranged, don't you?"

He nodded. "GPD's talked with the parents. Watson told me they were practically on his doorstep this morning."

"Well, I had breakfast with Jeffrey yesterday, and he told me about Rodman Dam."

"He told you? You mean you didn't know about it?"

"It's a long story, but I was in another world when my mother had her second stroke. Anyway, a couple of the Earth Save members I've been talking to seem frightened by Kincaid's death, and now by Becky's disappearance."

"I'm not surprised," he said, as he took a sip from the bottle of beer. "I told you it was possibly related to other cases being investigated in the area."

"Right, but here's my question: do you think Earth Save was involved in any way with the dam being blown up?"

He raised his eyebrows, shrugged, and gave me a look as though to say, *could be.*

"But I thought they'd been cleared by the FBI and others," I said.

"Cleared? Lorelei, the investigation is still underway. No one is cleared until there's solid evidence as to who committed the crime."

I considered what Homer said, and it made me angry. I stood up and walked across the room to face him.

"Homer McBride, did you intentionally manipulate me to gather information from Earth Save members? You do think they were the ones responsible for the sabotage, don't you?"

"Wait a minute," he protested. "I didn't manipulate anybody. You came to me, and you asked to be let in on the investigation. You wanted information about Kincaid's murder, remember?" He leaned forward, and put down his bottle of beer.

My voice felt tight as I responded. "I asked to let me help you only because Becky and Jeffrey were concerned—as friends—about the murder. They didn't know what was being done to solve it. You led me to believe there was some crazy person out to kill environmental activists. You never told me what you were really after was information about Rodman. I didn't even know about the dam at that point. You used me, Homer, and I don't like it one bit. I thought we had a more honest relationship."

Homer stood facing me, and touched my arm a placating way. "I'm sorry, Lorelei. I couldn't tell you everything. It might have impaired your ability to appear objective when you were asking questions."

I jerked my arm away from him, and returned to the couch. "Homer, I'm an actress, dammit. I can play anything—with or without a script. What in hell were you thinking?"

"I really didn't think you'd find out anything from them about Rodman anyway. Hell, they've already been grilled about it. If none of us could get anything on them, I didn't think you could. But if you actually did, why then it..."

"Then it what?" I retorted, my anger feeding on itself. "It would be a coup for the sheriff's office? Make the state and Feds look like you guys were on top of things? I've read about the competition among law enforcement agencies."

"No, it wasn't like that. Look, you asked me to let you poke around. I didn't think it could hurt, and there was a long shot it might yield information helpful in one case, or the other. Mostly though, it was more like doing you a favor."

"Some favor," I said.

We sat in silence for several moments; not looking at one another. It was as though neither one of us was willing to speak first to test the emotional waters.

Finally, I turned to him and said, "I'm really disappointed in you. After all we've been through together, and you still don't trust me with the complete truth." Jeffrey was right in forbidding me to even mention his suspicions to anyone else, least of all McBride.

"Lorelei, you don't really know what you've gotten yourself into. Whoever bombed Rodman is a terrorist just as if he or they worked for Al Qaeda."

"Now who's being dramatic? Al Qaeda, my foot."

"C'mon now, you said you've been talking to some Earth Save members. What have you found out?"

"Nothing, absolutely nothing. You can do your own damn investigating." I felt hurt and resentful at being used by him.

"Please, Lorelei," he coaxed.

"No. In fact, I think it's time you left."

"What about the pizza?" he said, looking with disappointment toward the kitchen. "You can take it, or leave it. I don't care." I stood up. "Now, I'm tired and I need to rest. Please just go."

He sighed, slowly stood up, and I followed him to the door. Before opening the door, he turned and suddenly kissed me. It was a hard kiss on the lips that lasted only a moment. I was too stunned to protest and, before I could say anything, he was gone. I walked into the kitchen and, despite the tantalizing aroma of pizza, decided I wasn't hungry anymore. As I undressed for bed, I thought, so much for my fantasy evening with Homer McBride. As usual, it was a might have been.

Chapter 12

The storm had cleared by the beginning of the week. Despite her claustrophobia, Becky made it through the dark and rainy days. Minerva's herbal remedies helped, as did an occasional walk outside the tent. Minerva provided a calming distraction by her insistence on Becky's participation in chanting and guided meditation sessions. They ate little and managed to sleep well, as though they were hibernating creatures awaiting spring.

After the storm, they worked at cleaning up the campsite, and restoring everything as it had been. Becky was glad for the physical activity. It kept her from brooding about her failed memory. Along with assisting the older woman, she set up a new latrine and, while she was in the woods, gathered small branches set to dry out in the sun. Fortunately, Minerva already had a supply of dry kindling which she kept wrapped in a tarpaulin behind the tent.

Late Tuesday afternoon, they sat outside in front of the small fire pit. It was used both to cook food and to smudge the area with smoke to kept the mosquitoes at bay. Minerva learned this method from a book she read on early Florida Indians who often lived in mosquito filled swamps.

"I know so little about you," Becky said. "We've spent what seems like weeks together, and I still don't know how you came to live out here." By this time, Becky was reassured the woman was not a mental case, as she had earlier feared. Indeed, Minerva seemed highly competent and rational.

"Isn't it interesting how threatening events force us to be present oriented, and to find kinship with strangers?" she said, slumped in her chair and staring into the fire. "My journey to this place isn't a pleasant one. I'm a fifty-nine year old woman on my own. Other than Fritz here, I've got no family except a very old aunt and uncle who live in California."

"I think your life is fascinating," Becky said. "I mean, all the things you know about taking care of yourself in the wild. I don't have a clue about myself, or where I've come from. It might help to know something about your life."

Minerva leaned over the side of the chair and patted Fritz. "Well, what do you say my friend? Shall we tell this young woman my dreary tale?" She gave Becky an inquiring look. "By the way, how about choosing a name for yourself while you're here? Minerva is a name I've chosen. It would be better if I could call you by something other than 'dear'".

"Choose a name?" Becky thought a moment, and decided she liked the idea. "Diana," she replied, surprising herself. "Yes, it's the first name that came to me. It even has a familiar feeling to it."

"Ah, Diana the huntress. You chose well considering you made your way through a wild part of the creek. It's very near the headwaters, you know. I've hiked it myself, and have seen its steep mossy walls, old oak trees, and dense overgrowth. You're lucky we found you when we did. Anyway, Diana, what is it about me you would like to know?"

Hearing herself called by name had a liberating effect on Becky. She felt a lightness of heart for the first time since arriving at the camp. Now, she thought, she was a somebody.

"What I'd like to know?" Becky considered Minerva's invitation. "First of all, who were you before you came to live like this—homeless, I mean."

Minerva laughed. "Homeless? Well, you might say I'm only sort of homeless. I've got a more or less settled place to be—until someone comes along and makes me move—and at least there's a tarp over my head, which is more than some have. But I certainly didn't choose to live like this. It happened gradually."

Becky turned her chair to face Minerva, and looking straight up to the west noticed the most breathtaking sky. It was a majestic flood of deep hues of red, orange, and pink spread like wide swaths of paint on a huge canvass. As she inhaled, she was aware of how fresh the air smelled after the cleansing storm. Everything seemed renewed.

Minerva, noticing the look of pleasure on Becky's face, said, "Sometimes, when I witness a sky like this one, I forget I'm homeless. I often sit out here in the early morning or evening, and I experience a kind of joy I never felt when I was living in a house, in the city, and working all the time."

Becky slapped her neck, and said. "Even with the mosquitoes?"

Minerva fanned the fire a bit, and reached under her chair to hand Becky a small jar with aloe.

"Here rub some of this on your neck and arms. Yes, I try enjoying every beautiful thing and each new experience—they all have a price of one sort or another."

"Are you telling me you actually enjoy living in a tent rather than in a nice home?"

Minerva studied Becky for a moment before answering.

"Like I said, only sometimes. Naturally, it would be ideal to have a house in the country—a permanent place to live with all the conveniences like a bathroom, electricity, and heat. But there are homeless people—like some of the vets with PTSD—who choose to live this way."

"PTSD?"

"Post traumatic stress disorder. It's an anxiety disorder. My friend, Tully, a Vietnam vet, says he can't live anywhere where he feels closed in. You'll meet him later."

"That's how I was feeling during the storm," Becky said. "Sometimes, it was like suffocating, and I don't feel like I'm sleeping—just kind of half awake. Do you think I have PTSD?"

"Maybe," Minerva said. "You certainly had a severe head injury, and obviously suffered a trauma great enough to land you in the creek in the condition you were in. But don't worry; I'm sure your memory will come back."

Becky reflected on this while Minerva got up to stir the fire. "Well, I guess I'll just have to be Diana, for now. You said it was a long journey that brought you here. Can you tell me about it?"

"I was raised in California. My parents moved to Jacksonville when I went to college here."

"Here being…?"

"The University of Florida. I graduated UF and moved back to Jacksonville. I went to work for a social service agency, and cared for my parents until they died."

"Were you married?"

"Yes, after my parents were gone, I married their accountant. We had dated for several years. We had a daughter together."

"Where is she now?" Becky asked.

Minerva looked away. "She was killed in an auto accident while my husband was taking to her soccer game. She was only nine."

Becky reached over to touch Minerva's hand. "Oh, I'm so sorry. What a terrible loss."

Minerva grew reflective and her voice softened. "It all went downhill after that. He began to drink and gradually he lost his clients. What happened next was pretty predictable."

"What do you mean?" Becky asked.

The older woman leaned forward and poked a stick at the fire before responding. "What happened is what's happened to a lot of homeless people. It's like backing down on a stepladder— you drop one step at a time and don't see you're headed for a fall, or hit bottom until it's too late."

Becky waited patiently and, in a few minutes, the woman continued her story.

"We got behind in our mortgage payments. At first, he left a lot of his earnings at the local bar, and then he started gambling. He foolishly thought he could win back the money he lost. We tried living on my salary. It wasn't enough. Then, he started getting violent with me."

"Oh, how terrible," Becky said, searching the woman's face for any signs of injury.

"I was embarrassed to go into work with bruises on my face— no, they're gone now," she said, seeing Becky's concern. "Anyway, I was absent a lot. The bank foreclosed on our house, and we moved into a cheap apartment. I had trouble keeping up with my caseload at work. We really reached bottom when I was laid off. The excuse was the state cutbacks, but I didn't blame them. I was pretty beat up by then—in every respect."

The woman gave a mirthless laugh, and said, "Sounds like your daytime soap opera doesn't it? But it's all true."

"Minerva, how terrible. I can understand why you left Jacksonville but, with your education and experience, surely you could have gotten a job here."

"You would think so. But I felt like a total failure and, in many ways, I still do. I mean, after all, I was a social service professional who couldn't even help her own husband, or herself. All the training and experience didn't prevent me from landing right here, in a tent."

They sat in silence for awhile as the brilliant flaming sky dimmed and turned purple and gray.

Finally, Becky asked, "Wouldn't you be better off in town where you'd be with other people?"

"I thought that, at first," she said, smiling sadly. "I tried one of the tent camps in town for awhile. At night it's noisy, there was a lot of garbage around, and I wasn't comfortable being a woman alone. Some nights there were drunken men roaming the camp. It didn't feel safe. Though I'll admit, some of the nicest people I ever met were also living there. They were just regular people down on their luck. They'd lost their jobs, got behind in their bills, and lost their housing. They were trying to get into Section 8 housing and find work. I even tried to help some of them since I knew the system."

"I'm sure you helped them a lot," Becky said. "Just like you've done for me."

"I sure tried. Then one day I got to talking with Tully. He was helping serve soup, to homeless people, on the downtown plaza. He told me about this land up here, and helped me move. I'm convinced this is the best place for me right now. I get a state pension so I can afford to buy some luxuries—just not enough to rent an apartment. Maybe when I get my Social Security I'll be able to afford housing."

"Don't you get terribly lonely?" Becky asked.

"I've gotten used to it. Fritz is an excellent companion and watch dog—a woman alone needs a dog."

Fritz, hearing his name, stood up next to Minerva and wagged his tail. She patted him, and said, "We're good together aren't we, buddy?"

After they watched the fire for a time, Minerva stood up and stretched. "It's about to get dark. Let's go into the tent. Tomorrow afternoon, we'll go to the downtown Farmers Market, and I'll find you some medical attention."

"How will we get to town?" Becky asked, looking at Minerva's bike parked alongside the tent.

"No, not on my handlebars," she said, and laughed. "My friend, Tully. He's just down the road a bit. When I get tired of that solar shower thing over there he lets use the one in his trailer." She pointed to the large gray plastic bag, which they had filled in the creek, and hung from a tree limb. "And he lets me use his stove to cook up some basics for the week. Things would be even rougher if it weren't for him. Anyway, he has an old truck, and he takes me to town when I need to go in. He'll take us."

They snuffed out the pit fire, and went into the tent. They both read for awhile by the light of the lantern. Minerva had given Becky a small book about Buddhism. She felt comforted by a quote from the woman Buddhist priest, Pema Chodron. She had written the goal in life was to have the courage to accept and welcome whatever appears—"sickness, health, poverty, wealth, sorrow, and joy." Becky tried meditating on letting go of her anxiety and questions about her identity. Despite it all, she continued to awaken with heart pounding terror during the night.

The next afternoon, the two women and the dog walked through the woods to Tully's. They approached a small trailer, which had a canopy attached to the side and tarps rolled up to be released in bad weather. It appeared to be outfitted like a living area—with a carpet, plastic lawn chairs, a sink and shaving table, a cook stove, and even a clock affixed to a post. Fritz ran ahead to the door of the trailer and started barking. A tall Black man emerged, bent to pet the dog and gave him a large bone.

"Fritz, my boy, how're you doin' today, fella? I saved this one just for you," he said, in a pleasing resonant voice. The man stood up, and with a big smile on his face, said, "Minerva, you're looking none the worse for the storm. I was thinking maybe I should go over and invite you to stay in the trailer, but I know you like to take care of yourself. I figured you'd come along if you needed." He glanced at Becky, but showed no surprise at her presence.

"Thank you, Tully. You're always so thoughtful. I want you to meet my new friend, Diana."

"How'd you do, Diana," he said, and extended his hand.

"Fritz and I found Diana in the creek a few days ago. She's been staying with us."

"In the creek?" he repeated. "Lord, girl, what were you doing in this end of Hogtown Creek?"

Becky immediately liked the man. He had a kindly face, and looked to be in his late fifties or sixties with a sprinkling of white hair at his temples. "I don't know," she said. "Thank goodness Minerva found me. I don't remember how I got there."

Tully gave Minerva a quizzical look.

"She's had quite an experience," Minerva said, pointing to Becky's head. "Got a real bad head wound. She was a mess when we found her. Anyway, we'd appreciate a lift downtown. I want to take Diana to the Helping Hands free clinic, and go to the farmer's market. Can you drive us?"

"Sure, I'll be happy to. You leaving Fritz here?"

The dog had already snuggled into a depression under the edge of the trailer, and was chewing on the bone Tully had given him.

Minerva said, "He'll be okay. He knows his way home, and he's very resourceful."

They left for downtown Gainesville in Tully's old red Ford truck. He took them to the library where Minerva said she wanted to return some books. They agreed to meet Tully back at the library in two hours.

As the two women walked toward the entrance to the Alachua County Library, Becky noticed the homeless men who lined the outside benches. Minerva saw her looking at them, stopped and said, "The library and the downtown plaza are a few of the places a homeless person can go, and not be forced to leave. Can you imagine what it's like being out on the streets all of the time?"

"It must be terrible," Becky replied. "Where do they even go to the bathroom?"

"Good question," Minerva said. "It's a big problem—especially in the evening when even the library is closed. There's also the question of where to keep their few possessions safe. Because lugging them around all day is a sure giveaway that you're homeless, and that invites all sorts of other problems. And where can they stay and sleep in rainy or freezing weather without being arrested for trespassing?"

"At least they'd have shelter in the jail," Becky said.

"And a nice police record to keep them from getting a job. Which is almost impossible anyway when you don't have a phone, a car, and haven't a place to bathe and clean up. Gainesville has so little room in its homeless shelters, and there's really no substitute for permanent decent housing. The local government tries to help, but they haven't significantly improved the situation. As a former social worker, I understand the complexities of housing the homeless."

Becky glanced again at the disheveled looking men who were sitting on the library benches.

Minerva said, "Yes, they look shabby. But the public only sees those out on the street. It's what gives them a negative stereotype about all homeless people—most of whom are hidden from view. They're living in tents, like me, or in cars, or crowded in with friends and relatives. Tully told me about a homeless man who was living, on Greyhound buses, by traveling continuously on his senior's bus pass. The only real difference between most of the homeless people and everybody else is that everybody else has permanent housing they can afford."

Becky sympathized with Minerva's anger and frustration. Yet, not until this moment, did she realize she, too, had become one of the hidden homeless.

Minerva dropped off her books, and they walked, from the library, to the free clinic which was also downtown. After only a short wait, a nurse volunteer examined Becky's head wound, and was satisfied to find it clean and beginning to heal. Becky and Minerva related how Becky was found. The nurse agreed with Minerva's assessment that Becky had some of the symptoms associated with PTSD. She told Becky that, in time, her memory would begin to come back. She suggested a return to the clinic, the following week, when the psychologist would be available. Becky was disappointed that nothing more could be done to aid her recovery. Minerva reassured her she could stay with her for as long as she needed to do so.

They returned to the downtown plaza, where the weekly farmer's market was in progress, and browsed the many stalls. There were a variety of vegetable and fruit vendors. People were also selling baked goods, homemade clothing, jewelry, candles, and preserves, plants, organic dairy products, coffee, and herbs. Though she couldn't identify why, Becky had a feeling of familiarity with the place and its colorful diversity of people and goods. There were young and old people of various ethnicities, families, well dressed professionals on their way home from work, students, hippies, and homeless people— all mingling together. A carnival atmosphere was further created by a band playing folk music on the plaza stage.

Minerva purchased some organic vegetables and a couple of herb plants. She treated Becky to a pastry at one of the bakery stands, and they stood nearby eating the delicious baked goods.

Becky noticed a woman, on the opposite side of the booth, who was staring—wide-eyed and open-mouthed—directly at her. Finally, she watched as the woman rushed over, and planted herself directly in front of Becky.

"Becky Haimovitz! Where have you been? Everybody's looking for you. Even your parents are here, and they're beside themselves with worry."

Chapter 13

I was thrilled by the news that Becky had been found. It was close to midnight when Jeffrey called. He said he had only just heard about it from a mutual friend. I wanted to see Becky, but he said her parents planned to whisk her home, to Boston. They were leaving on the first morning flight out of Gainesville—which I knew to be six or seven a.m. He also told me that Becky was suffering amnesia, and probably wouldn't even recognize me. I called Delcie immediately after talking with him.

"Hi, Del. Sorry to call so late, but I knew you'd want to hear this. Guess who finally turned up?" I said.

"Becky?"

"Yes. Apparently, her friend Candace—the one with the cats—spotted her at the downtown farmer's market this afternoon. Jeffrey just called to tell me about it."

"The farmer's market? What in the world was she doing there?"

"I don't know. She was with an older homeless woman, and when Candace came up to them, Becky didn't even recognize her."

"Uh oh," Delcie said.

"Right. Candace called the police right away. The homeless woman told the police she found Becky, barely conscious, in the Hogtown Creek up near the headwaters."

"So that's where she went to."

"Yes, she's been staying at the woman's campsite and, according to Candace, Becky had no recollection of what happened to her, or how she wound up in the creek."

"Well, I could take a guess about what happened, couldn't you? Given how we found her car, we can assume someone scared her enough to chase her into the creek. Only Becky can tell us who it was and what happened. That is, when she remembers. From what you've said, sounds like she's in shock."

"You're right," I said, and I had a flash that whoever chased Becky was the same person or persons who may have killed Stoker. "Anyway, the sad thing is, from what Jeffrey told me, Becky looked terrified when the police arrived and wanted her to go with them to her parent's hotel. She didn't want to leave the older woman, but they finally persuaded her."

"Poor Becky," Delcie said. "At least she'll get good medical treatment at home. Losing your memory like that is scary."

"Until she recovers, we're stuck without an answer to who is stalking Earth Save members, and why."

"Well, that's too much mystery this late at night, Lorelei. I'm glad Becky's been found, and is safe. Now, I've got to give up watching Dave Letterman and get some sleep. I suspect you do as well. Call me if you hear something more, and let's plan dinner one night this week."

"Sounds good, goodnight Del," I said, and stretched out in bed feeling wide awake. I considered whether to get up and do some relaxing yoga postures, or just pop a pill. The pill won.

For the next two weeks, I focused all my time and energy on *Sweeney Todd*. I had not heard from Homer since our falling out on pizza night, and Jeffrey had gone to Costa Rica for a month. I made weekly calls to my mother, and Delcie was the only non-theater friend with whom I socialized. Neither one of us heard any news about the Kincaid investigation.

Jeffrey had given me the number for Becky's parents, and I called them a couple of times to see how she was doing. They told me her memory was starting to return. She was under the care of a psychiatrist. They asked that if I learned anything about what happened to her in Gainesville, to call them as it might hasten her recovery. They didn't offer to let me talk with her, and I didn't force the issue.

With Becky's safety assured and Jeffrey out of town, I was no longer absorbed by Kincaid mystery. After the 4th of July, rehearsals became more intense in advance of the September opening. My social life revolved around fellow cast members. We hung out at the theater, had potluck dinners at Renee's house, or drinks at a little bar and grill on SW 16ᵗʰ Avenue.

I was experiencing the luxury of living wholly for the theater, without having to shift my focus for another relationship, a job, or—as it was in Apalachicola—a full scale murder investigation with Homer McBride.

Jeremy Hastings and I began getting to know one another better as a natural consequence of long hours rehearsing and after hours socializing. We were the only two actors in the cast who were about the same age, and the fact that we were both single offered grist for conversation. We swapped stories about our acting experiences. Like me, he had given New York a chance to discover him, as he put it, before returning to the regional theater circuit. We talk about the many things we found in common. One subject, which came up often, was the conviction that being in the theater was the only enduring passion in our lives.

Late one evening, after a particularly arduous rehearsal, Jeremy and I agreed to break away and go to a downtown restaurant. It wasn't like a date, but it was the first time we were together without other cast members. The summer heat was blasting Gainesville, as only those who remain here during July and August well know. Yet this evening there was a light breeze—it was almost balmy—and we chose to dine al fresco at a sidewalk table. The piped music was soft Brazilian jazz .

I ordered the soup du jour and Jeremy selected a tapas plate. We agreed to share a bit of each. After a few sips of wine I began feeling very relaxed. In the glow of candlelight, I found myself observing him with more interest than at any time previous. As he talked about a recent visit to Puerto Rico and his taste for Latin food, I found myself once more transfixed by his pale blue eyes made bluer in contrast to their black pupils. I scanned his face, and enjoyed seeing the half smile that broke when he paused to glance at a passerby. His long slender fingers held the wine glass lightly, with the assurance of someone who has spent many hours in café's, lingering over a single glass of wine. He was the most elegant man I'd ever met.

"It was good tonight, wasn't it?" he said, abruptly changing the subject to work. Looking at my hair, he added, "I meant to tell you how much I like the way you've had your hair cut."

I reflexively reached up to brush it back from my face. "Really, you like it short? I had it cut to fit under the bakers cap."

"In the cap, not so attractive. Otherwise, it's beautiful, long or short," he said, with a look of approval.

"Why, thank you, Jeremy," I replied, surprised by the hint coquetry in my voice.

I looked away to break the spark of energy between us, and thought oh, my God, I'm flirting with him. It's this romantic setting. Yikes. Get a grip, Lorelei, or at the rate you're going, you'll be in his bed within ten minutes of leaving a tip for the waiter.

"What's wrong?" Jeremy asked, seeing my distracted look.

"Wrong? Nothing really. Except well, to tell the truth," I sputtered. "I'm just not ready to get involved with anyone right now."

He appeared to be taken aback, then laughed and gave me an amused, but affectionate look.

"Dear Lorelei, I thought you would have guessed by now."

"Guessed?" I said, and suddenly felt the heat rise from my neck into my face. "Oh, Jeremy, don't tell me you're gay."

"As a Franz Lehar operetta," he said.

"That's 'The Merry Widow'; not the 'Gay Divorcee,'" I replied.

"Guilty on both counts," he said, flicking his wrist in a caricature gay gesture.

I laughed and said, "No kidding, I am so embarrassed. I guess it was the music, the wine, and the candlelight. I'm a sucker for romantic scenes. Always have been."

"Me, too," he said, and glanced away to look at the young college students passing by on the sidewalk.

He saw me follow his glance and, with a sheepish look on his face, said, "Just looking. They're so beautiful when they're young, aren't they."

"Yes," I said. "Living in a college town is an exercise in wistfulness at the beauty and brevity of youth."

"Well put. But the life well lived eventually has its revenge on callow youth," he intoned, and raised his glass in a toast before sipping from it.

"My, aren't we waxing poetic. Speaking of revenge…"

Our meals arrived, the waiter retreated, and we continued talking.

"You were saying about revenge? You mean as the subject of our play?" he asked, offering me an artichoke from his plate. It was delicious.

I said, "I've been doing some research on revenge plays. Of course, I knew about the classics—Seneca and others. But I learned that early modern revenge plays were a very popular genre during the Elizabethan and Jacobean eras. It didn't begin with *Hamlet,* as I had thought. Did you ever hear of *The Spanish Tragedy*?"

"Heavens, yes. Have you never taken a drama history course? Thomas Kyd's play was a seminal work in England, and wildly popular for many years. Let's see, it was produced in the late 1500s, if I recall correctly. In fact, *Hamlet* is said to have advanced the complexity of the revenge play, but it was Kyd's formula that Shakespeare improved upon."

"So almost three hundred years later, in the mid-1800s, comes the very popular *Sweeney Todd*—which fits into this genre, don't you think?" I said. "And, we're still exploring the theme in the twenty-first century."

"How time flies," he replied, lifting his glass in a mock toast.

I continued, "Our play doesn't have all of Kyd's traditional elements, such as murdered rulers and ghostly visits. It is the kind of morality play which persists today, with characters who are innocent and pure, like Johanna, and evil ones like…"

"You and me," Jeremy said, wringing his hands with a diabolical look. "Oh, what fun to be evil? It's so much easier to play than being pure. Of course, I've gotten a couple of notes from Renee about indulging my pleasure in the role a bit too much. But revenge is such an interesting psychological phenomenon. I'm sure it will forever be our dramatic métier."

"Just look at the daily news," I added. "It's filled with violent revenge by individuals and even nations. It's obviously a universal part of our psychology."

The waiter returned to clear our table and deliver a check. Jeremy reviewed the bill and placed money inside the black folio. "Keep it," he told the man, who bowed slightly and thanked him.

"So what you're suggesting is a kind of drive for revenge, like sex and food?" he asked, leaning his elbows on the cleared table. "I guess we do seem to have an appetite for it when we've been harmed. But then, how do you explain forgiveness? What about the person who seems genuinely to forgive someone who harms him—kills his child or something horrible like that?"

I thought for a moment. "I guess I would have to say that forgiveness must be an attribute of higher consciousness. At least it's what all the religions seem to preach as a spiritual goal."

"Oh yeah," Jeremy said. He gave me a skeptical look, and folded his napkin into a neat square. "Those same religions which have forever been killing one another in their so-called holy wars. Uh huh, big on tolerance and forgiveness are they?"

I shrugged, looked at the time on Jeremy's watch, and saw it was almost midnight. I pushed back my chair and said, "We'd better get going. I have an early fitting tomorrow. It's been a lovely evening, Jeremy. Thanks so much."

"My pleasure, Lorelei. Actually, I was feeling a bit at loose ends here. You know how it is for an actor in a strange town. Now I feel I at least have one friend."

"You do, and I hope we can do this again—without the kids," I said, jokingly referring to our young colleagues. We got up from the table.

He laughed. "The students are fun. I really enjoy working with them, and listening to how they communicate with one another."

"When they're not texting or twittering," I said, as we walked out of the restaurant to the street. We stood at the curb in front of my car.

"Oh yes, twitters and tweets," he said. "What's the rush for all this communication? Everyone seems to be time-stressed—like

Alice's white rabbit. I'll have to admit I'm way behind the tech curve. Anyway, it feels good to have someone around my own age to talk to. Renee puts me off for some reason, Alex Champion sticks to himself, and of course Rick…"

"He does get a bit dramatic, doesn't he?" I said. "Maybe he should return to acting."

"Yes, but you'd better suggest it. He'd ice me if I did. So, it's goodnight, Lorelei. See you tomorrow." He gave me a brief kiss on the cheek, turned and walked away to his car which was parked farther down the street.

Driving back to my condo, I reflected on our conversation about revenge. I was convinced it was not only central to our play, but also the likely motive for Adam Kincaid's murder. It was the reference made, by both Tim and Bear, to the Rodman Dam that convinced me. Someone was taking revenge on Gainesville activists in the belief they were responsible for blowing the dam. By the time I pulled into the garage of my condo, I knew I would have to break the ice and call Homer in the morning.

Chapter 14

I was standing at the kitchen counter, sipping the last of my morning tea, when I put in a call to Homer at the Sheriff's Office.

"Lorelei? What a surprise. When I didn't hear from you the past couple of weeks, I thought..."

"What did you think, Homer?" I said. "I mean, I'm still a bit steamed at how you played me."

"Now, Lorelei, I can see how you must have thought that but, at the time, I really did believe I was giving you something you wanted. I'm sorry it didn't turn out that way."

"Well, let's not rerun it. I'll admit I might have overreacted. I accept your apology," I remembered his earnest kiss at the doorway which attempted to transcend our fractious parting. "Now you can make it up to me."

"Sure, how about dinner and we can start over."

"Maybe another evening, Homer. Right now I'm not free in the evenings. I would like an update on the Kincaid investigation, and Becky's disappearance."

"Sorry, Lorelei, I can't do that."

"Can't, or won't?" I asked, wondering if I'd made a mistake in forgiving him so easily.

"I'm not on the case anymore."

"What? Have you been demoted, or something?"

He laughed, "No nothing like that. Remember all the advanced training I took in Tallahassee last year? Well, the day after I saw you, I found out I'd been assigned to a major computer fraud case. It's taking all of my time."

"Really? That sounds interesting. So, who can I ask about the Kincaid case?"

"You can try Detective Kyle Watson, at GPD."

"Like the Sherlock Holmes Watson?" I asked.

"Yes, but don't kid him about it, or you'll never get anything out of him."

"Okay then, if I call Detective Watson can I use your name? Will you vouch for me?"

"I will, if you promise not to tell him about your involvement with my investigations. That's our secret."

I'll bet, I thought. "Okay, I promise. I'll act like we're just old acquaintances."

"And don't expect too much from him. He's a stickler for procedure. As I think about it, I'll be surprised if he'd reveal anything to you."

"Great, so I shouldn't bother. Homer, you must have heard something even if you're not still on the case."

"The only thing I know is Watson's concluded it was a drug deal gone bad. When Kincaid's apartment was searched they found a stash of marijuana, some coke and a lot of cash."

"You never told me about that," I said. "A drug deal? I don't think so. I'm certain it was related to the Rodman dam."

He laughed. "Same old, Lorelei. So, you're back in the detective business. You sure you're not confusing Kincaid with one of Sweeney Todd's victims? By the way, in your honor, I watched the movie again on Netflix. Not bad the second time, but I still don't think I want Bobby to see it."

"No, don't be silly. I'm not confusing anything. It just adds up after what I've learned."

"You're not withholding evidence I hope. That wouldn't sit well with Watson. It never did with me either."

It didn't occur to me my conclusion about the case might be without merit. On the contrary, I was baffled that Watson arrived at something entirely different. And, I wondered why no one I talked to had ever mentioned that Stoker was heavily involved in drug trafficking. Jeffrey certainly didn't think so.

I still wasn't going to divulge my conversations with Bear and Tim. Instead I reminded Homer of what he told me. "When we had our little set-to it was you who mentioned the significance of the Rodman. I happen to think it's central to the Kincaid case."

He said, "And you may be right, but it's Watson's call. Anyway, how about having dinner with me in about a week or so?"

"Yes, Homer. I'd like that." And I meant it. Talking with him made me realize how nice it would be to renew our relationship, but not just yet.

When the conversation ended, I put my cup in the sink and left for my costume fitting. On the way to the theater, I thought about our conversation. From what Homer said, I guessed it would be futile to seek help from Watson. Yet, more than ever, I felt I owed it to Becky—and her recovery—to learn the truth. I would simply have to investigate on my own. If matters got sticky, Delcie would help me.

Where to begin? I remembered Jeffrey giving me the name of a Putnam County environmentalist who knew a lot about the dam and could take me around. Talking to her would be the most logical place to start since I believed what had happened in Gainesville was linked to the Kirkpatrick dam.

I called Delcie, but got her voice mail. I left word I was going to Palatka the next day, and wanted to have dinner with her when I returned. I expected I'd have a lot to tell her. I said I'd call when I got back into town, and I suggested we meet at Ivey's on University. It was one of our favorite places for dinner.

Sharon Adelle was free after lunch, and we agreed to meet at a small coffee shop on the main street in Palatka. She was the only one seated when I arrived at 1:30. She didn't fit my image of an environmental activist. Sharon was a slender woman with a pleasant round face, a creamy complexion and steely gray eyes. I guessed her to be around my age, in her mid-forties. When she went to the counter to order our coffees, I was struck by the way she was dressed. I noticed she was wearing a cool looking North Face outfit—long sleeved white blouse, taupe convertible pants and matching colored Merrill sandals. Her brunette ponytail stuck out the back of a tan baseball cap with a Sierra Club emblem. Sharon's overall appearance said Junior League, rather than the League of Conservationists.

She returned to the table, and said, "On the phone you mentioned you once worked for the Center for Earth Options in Gainesville. They've been very supportive of our efforts here in Putnam County."

"Yes, I remember, but it's been a long time since I worked for them. Actually, I've been away from the region awhile. Jeffrey told me about Rodman, uh, I mean Kirkpatrick Dam."

She winced at the mention of the name.

"He said Putnam County environmentalists do a terrific job. I guess now you're fighting the water management district's plan to pipe water, out of the Ocklawaha and St. Johns rivers, to other counties."

She sighed. "We do have a full plate. But we have a lot of help from friends like Jeffrey, and the support of other environmental groups. Of course, now the spillway has been partially breeched, we're hoping the river will gradually return to a normal flow. It would help if they removed the concrete, but that's another battle. Hopefully, the legislature will find it too expensive to repair. Anyway, you'll see what I mean when we go out there."

I was eager to get going. When I glanced up at the wall clock, Sharon said, "I'm ready whenever you are. We don't have to hang around here. We can talk on the way."

She waved a goodbye to the young woman tending the counter, and we left the café.

"Let's take my car," she said. "Its right here—the olive Honda. Where did you park?"

"In a lot by the church," I said, pointing in its direction.

"Good, it'll be fine until we return."

She clicked open the doors to the small sports utility vehicle, we got in, and started on our way to the river.

I wanted to learn more about Sharon, and asked the first question that struck me. "Where are you from, originally? I detect a Midwestern accent."

She laughed. "I'm from Michigan. I met my husband at Ann Arbor."

"So, what brought you to Putnam County?" For some reason, I was always curious about what made people move to North Central Florida.

"My husband did. He was born in Palatka, and when he graduated from law school and we married...well, his father wanted him to join the family law practice. So here we settled."

"A bit of culture shock for you," I said.

"Tell me about it. I've lived here for more than twenty years, but every time I meet someone new, they ask, 'where y'all from?' Just like you did."

"Yes, I've heard many people in Putnam County are pretty aware of who's kin and who isn't. It's kind of a Southern thing. I'm surprised you've made so much headway in your environmental work. You do have several strikes against you, don't you?"

"The biggest one around here is the Ocklawaha restoration. Sometimes I think it'd be safer to put a 'Pro Life' bumper sticker on my car than one in favor of restoring the river."

"No kidding, people are that much against it?"

"Against is a mild description. It's an extremely emotional issue. So much so, I always alert the police when we have any type of public event. We worry it could get violent."

We drove out of Palatka. About ten minutes later, Sharon pulled off in front of a river outfitter's shop with canoes and kayaks displayed in the yard.

"We'll get a canoe from Pops Logan. I used to have a canoe, but we only use kayaks now."

We got out of the car and entered the small trailer that served Logan's Outfitters. Sharon chatted with the old man about the weather, and told him we wanted a canoe for a couple hours. He called to another man, Lonnie, who appeared at the door of the trailer, and instructed him to load a canoe onto Sharon's SUV.

I whipped out my credit card and insisted upon paying for the canoe.

"After all," I said. "I'm the one who asked for this excursion. It's your time; let it be my money."

She smiled and said, "Thanks."

When we approached the car, Lonnie looked at me kind of funny.

"Do I know you?" I asked, suddenly thinking he looked familiar. He wore a hat—I've heard it called a bucket hat—wrap-around sunglasses, and a pair of worn denim overalls.

"No m'am, I don't guess so," he said, turning his back to us as he began strapping the canoe to the rails atop her car. "Goin' out on the river to look at the dam? We get lots of folk wantin' to see it now that it's busted."

"Uh huh," Sharon replied absently, and motioned me into the car. "Thanks for your help," she said.

The man stepped away, but I watched him in the side view mirror as he continued to look at us even when we started down the road. I still had a funny feeling I knew him from somewhere. Lonnie? The name didn't ring any bells.

"Lorelei, there's some sunscreen in my bag if you need it, and an extra cap on the back seat."

"Good idea," I said, "I'll take you up on the sunscreen. I don't much like caps." It was a typically hot sunny day, but I hadn't thought about protecting myself. I guessed sunscreen and the hat was what kept Sharon's skin so lovely.

We kept driving for awhile, passed over a small trestle bridge, and turned into an area that looked like it was used by boaters. It had a path leading to a low bank where it would be easy to put a boat into the water. The area was vacant except for a couple of cars parked in the shade of a large live oak tree. I helped her unload the canoe and we walked it down to the river.

We shoved off into the water and began paddling in silence. It was a relatively narrow passage with grasses along the bank and a canopy of forest trees and shrubs in shades of green and brown. The air was a buzz with bird sounds and the hum of cicadas. There was a refreshing breeze as we glided along in the center of the gently winding river.

Finally, she broke the silence. "I wanted you to experience the beauty of the river before you saw the dam and spillway. This is the way it looked before the Barge Canal construction. In a little while you'll see the straight wide channel that was cut leading to dam. When they built it, they destroyed thousands of acres of river floodplain forest. Archie Carr once said that the Ocklawaha was the most beautiful river in Florida. You can see why people love it so."

We drifted along for about a half an hour. Sharon called my attention to a row of turtles nesting on a sunny log and various birds—an anhinga, a great blue heron, some limpkins, and a family of wood ducks. It seemed to be a birder's paradise. We spied a large alligator, lying alongside a cypress tree. I was relieved when it didn't move as we passed by. I lifted my paddle and inhaled the woodsy aroma. Carr was right. It is a gorgeous place and deserved to be protected.

"Jeffrey told me a bit about the history," I said, turning to back to Sharon. "But when did they begin trying to restore the river?"

She answered, "Let's see, in the early 1960s, Marjorie Carr and Dr. David Anthony led Gainesville's Audubon Society in a 'Save the Ocklawaha' campaign. It was shortly after the federal government approved an appropriation to build the canal. A few years later, Carr led the formation of Florida Defenders of the Environment, and continued work to save the river. Finally, in 1971, the Cross Florida Barge Canal project was stopped by a federal injunction. Its potential environmental damage was clear. I guess it was about then that talk of restoration began."

I said, "That probably explains why supporters of the dam and reservoir might have hostility toward Gainesville environmentalists."

"Oh, you've got that right. Gainesville is not a popular place for a lot of folk around here. They think you all are troublemakers—ivy tower environmentalists—who don't mind your own business."

"Interesting perspective. In a way, I see their point." I said. "But what surprises me is restoration efforts have not taken place after all this time."

"That's right," she said. "It's all about politics. Some powerful state and national figures, and their constituents, keep finding creative ways to defeat restoration. It's hard to understand their opposition. The Ocklawaha is the St. Johns River's largest tributary, and it's just so outstanding in many ways."

"It's a wonder no one tried to breech the dam before this. My goodness, almost forty years since the Barge Canal was stopped?"

She started paddling again, and said, "Now, just around this bend, you'll see the spillway in the distance."

At that moment, a loud noise prompted me to look back. I saw a boat coming up behind us. It looked like a pontoon boat, and seemed to be running at a fast pace.

Sharon caught my glance and also turned. "Damn! At the speed he's going we'll be swamped unless he cuts the engine and swerves out of the way. Let's try to paddle over to the bank."

We both started paddling. When I turned to look again, the boat had closed the distance and was parallel to us. It had slowed and was drifting near us. The canoe started tipping from their wake. I grabbed hold of the sides, and leaned against the oncoming waves hoping to counteract their action.

I caught a glimpse of two men. Their heads were covered with black ski masks. As Sharon and I struggled to keep our canoe from tipping, I noticed the pontoon boat make a turn around and then head back toward us. This was getting scary, I thought—why were they masked?

"What are they up to?" Sharon yelled. "Keep a tight grip on your paddle. We'll try to get out of the damn wake."

I pushed and pulled on the paddle with all my might. My hands begin to burn. The canoe kept riding up and down in the waves generated by the pontoon boat. I shoved my feet under the tip of the canoe hoping to steady myself and held on for dear life. I was certain I'd be in the water in a moment. I found myself gasping for air—in a totally high stress mode. It was a crazy ride, and all I could do was to keep myself inside the canoe.

Sharon was still trying to paddle us out of the wake and toward shore when the pontoon boat came alongside. One of the men extended a pole with a hook on the end. He grabbed the bow of the canoe. When he pulled it closer to their boat the wave action pushed our stern away. The canoe began floating perpendicular to the pontoon boat, and riding up and down across the wake.

"What the hell...?" I screamed, and stood up. "Are you crazy?"

"Use your paddle," Sharon yelled from behind me. "Hit him. Push the canoe away."

But the canoe was now held firmly against their boat. Before I could free my paddle to respond, one of the men reached toward me and grabbed the neck of my shirt. He began pulling me up and along the side of the pontoon boat.

Sharon must have seen what was happening, and yelled, "Jump, Lorelei."

I twisted and fought against the man's grasp. He began swearing at me as my blouse started to rip. I lost my balance and the canoe tipped over.

Oh my God, I thought, sinking underwater. My mind screamed, *Alligators. Snakes.*

I came up gulping and spitting out water. I struggled to start swimming, but found myself thrashing in place like a dog thrown into the water.

"Don't let her get away," a man in the boat yelled.

A float board dropped in front of me. I grabbed it with what turned out to be a foolish attempt at safety. As soon as I wrapped my arms around the board, I felt it being yanked back against the boat by a rope attached to it.

I let go of the board, the boat slammed against me, and I ducked underwater once again.

When I came up, gasping for air, the two men grabbed me by my arms. They pulled me aboard, as if I were a large mackerel.

Once they had me on deck, they dumped me face down. I was in shock. I could barely catch my breath.

I heard the engine start up and felt the boat jerk forward. Sharon was yelling my name while one of the men, with his knee in my back, hogtied me. He rolled me over and, before he blindfolded me, I saw he was still wearing the ski mask. All I could see were his bloodshot eyes and puffy red lips.

"You're a pissy girl, all right," he said, breathing heavily, "But we landed you anyway, didn't we?"

I felt nauseated. My chest started heaving and, for an instant, I hoped I would retch on him. But he stuffed a rag in my mouth. A new fear inserted itself—that I would choke on my own vomit and die.

The man must have sensed my panic. He said, "Breathe through your nose. You'll be all right." His voice sounded oddly reassuring.

I caught a whiff of a chemical on the rag and his breath smelled of beer. I concentrated on breathing through my nose, and trying to regulate my breath to keep from hyperventilating. I will survive, I thought. I felt a sharp prick on my arm just before I drifted into unconsciousness.

Chapter 15

I was awakened by loud banging. I slowly opened my eyes and felt groggy. The banging stopped and I found myself lying atop a musty old fashioned cot in a darkened room. Without getting up, I looked around. I was able to see well enough by the shafts of light coming through small cracks in the wooden walls. In the corner, above me, a large cobweb shimmered in the light and I studied it for a moment. A large black spider was moving about as though my presence had put it on alert. Taking in the whole room, I guessed I was in a cabin that hadn't been used in a long time. The windows were boarded up with cobwebs covering them, and the wooden floor had a coating of dust.

To the right of the bed I saw a straight-backed cane chair, a small wooden table, and a large bucket. A roll of toilet paper, on the floor next to it, made clear its purpose.

Great, I'm in a monk's cell. At least it's still daylight, I thought, as I rubbed my sore wrists. I sat up on the edge of the cot, bent over, and massaged my bruised ankles. The noise started up again. The hammering was coming from the other side of the only door in the room.

"Hello?" I tried to shout, but my mouth was so dry I had trouble getting out the words. "Will you please come in here?"

I stared at the door, but there was no answer. When the hammering stopped, I heard the click of a bolt.

Oh my God, I thought. They've fixed a lock on the door. They must be planning on keeping me here for awhile.

I tried standing, but felt dizzy and dropped back down to the cot. My clothes were wet and sticking to me.

I pushed myself off the bed and went to the door. I pressed my body close to it listening for sounds. I heard a man's deep voice, but it was too far away for me to make out the words. He sounded angry.

123

I banged on the door and yelled, pushing my hoarse throat to the limit, "Could you at least get me some dry clothes and water. I'm thirsty."

Still no answer.

I returned to the cot, lay down, and considered my situation. I looked around the room again to see what I could use for an escape, or as a weapon against my jailers. The choices were limited and required a great deal of creativity if escape was the only option.

I reflected on why the men had taken me prisoner. Why not Sharon, or both of us? Thinking of Sharon made me hope she had been able to right the canoe and get safely back to shore. I knew she'd report what happened to the authorities and they would start looking for me. I had another thought; did the men who grabbed me want me in particular, or just any woman? I didn't even want to consider the possibility it was a random snatch, and I was being kept prisoner for other more terrifying reasons.

No, it was more likely because of my connection to...what? Earth Save? Stoker and Becky? Yet how would anyone in Putnam County know I was here and what I was seeking? In my mind's eye, I saw the man at the outfitter's—the one who looked so familiar. Where had I seen him before? Bingo, I knew it. He was the guy from Charley's who had been staring at me. Yeah, the chubby guy at the bar. I think he recognized me at Pop's Outfitters. He must have been the one to let the two men know we were going on the river. My head began to ache and the room felt oppressively stuffy.

"Breathe, Lorelei," I whispered.

I moved to the chair and turned it to face the door on the opposite wall. I closed my eyes and started taking slow, deep breaths. I thought, they'll have to come in eventually and I'll find out what they want. In the meantime, meditation and yoga. It's what gets me through everything.

It wasn't long before I heard the click of a bolt being pulled.

I remained seated and watched the door.

A slender youngish looking man entered the room. He wore the same ski mask I'd seen when they grabbed me. He closed the door and stood, as if hesitating, before fully entering the room.

I stared at him and said nothing.

He was wearing jeans and a faded black T-shirt that had "X-Men" written across it. Thankfully, he was carrying two bottles of water along with a sandwich baggie.

"Water," I said. "Please."

As he took a few steps toward me I noticed he had a slight limp.

He said, "I'll give you the water, but you have to let me blindfold you and tie your hands. Please don't try to fight me, or he'll come in and hurt you."

"Hurt me? Why?" I asked, and remembered the shock of being slammed on the deck of the pontoon boat and hogtied. Yes, whoever "he" referred to was definitely capable of hurting me.

The young man's voice was soft and his manner was non-aggressive. I trusted his warning. "Okay," I said. "I won't fight. Just give me the water."

He crossed the room, handed me one of the bottles of water and placed the other one on the table along with the sandwich.

"It's peanut butter and jelly in case you get hungry," he said.

I gulped down most of the water until I felt my mouth and body rehydrated.

I asked, "Who the hell are you guys, and why have you've brought me here?"

He took a piece of cloth from his back pocket. "He'll tell you," he said, fastening the blindfold around my eyes. He took the bottle from my hands and added, "Now, please put your hands behind the chair."

I did as he asked and felt my wrists being tied to the slats on the chair back.

"You don't seem like a kidnapper. Why are you doing this to me?"

He didn't answer. I heard the creak of the floor boards as he walked to the door.

Within a few minutes, I heard the door being opened. I could almost feel the change of energy in the room as the sound of heavy boots crossed the floor toward me.

"I hope you tied her good," said man in a gruff voice that was clearly different than his partner's. I caught the scent of tobacco, and heard the bedspring creak as he sat down next to me.

"Who are you? What do you want from me?" I demanded again.

"I'll ask the questions," he said. "And you'd better tell me the truth, or we'll leave here to rot."

"You don't frighten me," I replied, with more conviction than I felt. "My friend will have already reported you to the police. They'll be looking for me."

"Don't count on it," he said. "She didn't see much of anything definite. She was too busy trying not to drown." He let out a dry laugh.

"Well I'm sure if she couldn't describe you, at least she saw your boat. It had a name on it."

"Did it now?" he said, and I could imagine his face sporting a sly grin. "But let's forget about your friend. It's you I'm interested in. Tell me about your buddies at Earth Save."

"What do you mean?" I said. I actually felt relieved by his question since it confirmed a reason for my abduction.

"You know what I mean," he said. "You were in on it, weren't you?"

"In on what?"

"The bombing. You, Waterman, and the others. Now I want to know the names of the other ones who blew up the dam."

"If you're asking about the Rodman Dam, I don't know anything about who did it. And, I certainly wasn't involved. I was in South Florida when it happened."

"It doesn't make a difference. We ain't going to let no terrorists from Gainesville get away with it, and you've been seen with 'em. We know who some are. We want the names of the rest of 'em. They're going to pay for what they did. Justice must be done."

Terrorists? He apparently stood up, and was leaning toward me. I could feel his breath close to my face. It had the same mixture of beer and tobacco I remembered from the boat.

"So, you gonna tell us, or do I have to give you a reason?" he demanded.

I said, "There's nothing I can tell you. I don't know who demolished the dam. I just came out here to see it. I was curious. That's all."

The air in the room seemed to evaporate as I heard my involuntary scream. The loud thump on the floor was his boot—with my foot under it. My body ricocheted back against the desk and then fell sideways onto the cot. The pain was so intense I thought I would pass out.

"Jesus, J.T, why'd you do that?" I heard the voice of the young man.

"Shut up. She's lying. Did you forget our granddaddy was fishing on the river when it was blown up and was almost drowned.? I'm gonna make her tell us who did it, or she's never gonna leave here."

The man roughly pulled me and the chair upright. I was panting for several moments. So was this about their grandfather? I was confused—and terrified. Did he break my foot? I became totally absorbed by the pain.

Minutes passed before anyone spoke. I heard the lighter footsteps of the younger man leave the room and return.

"Here, this should keep it from swelling." It was the soft voice speaking. He was loosening the shoe on my left foot, and I felt something cold being placed on the opened flap.

"All right, Nurse Betty," the other man said, in a mocking voice. "Let's get on with it. I think she knows now that I mean business."

I began recovering from the shock and initial pain of the blow. "May I please have some water?" I asked, purposely affecting a submissive tone.

"Give it to her," the older man directed.

A bottle was held to my mouth and I drank from it, trying not to choke.

"Thank you," I said.

Being blindfolded and tied up was clearly a disadvantage in dealing with the older man. I decided my only strategy was to play to the younger one. At some point I might even make him an ally. He already seemed sympathetic to me.

"Now, let's see if you've changed your mind about telling us who blew up the dam." It was my interrogator speaking.

"I swear to you. I don't know anything about it. I wasn't even in North Florida when it happened."

"But we know you're in with the group that did it. So, you must know the names of the guilty ones. Or, would you like me to flatten your other foot, too."

Before I could respond, I heard the younger man say, "Don't. Leave her alone for awhile. Give her a chance to think about it."

There was a pause, and I hoped the older man would take the suggestion.

Finally, he said, "Okay, we'll give her time to consider whether or not she wants both her feet broken. You can untie her when I leave. She won't be going anywhere soon—if ever, unless she tells us what we want to know."

He obviously was trying to terrorize me, and it was working.

I heard the door close and, moments later, the younger man removed the blindfold and untied my hands. He was still wearing a ski mask.

"Lady, you'd better tell him what he wants," he whispered, "He can get real mean." With that said, he turned and left the room.

I dragged my injured foot to the door and tried to hear what they were saying.

The older man said, "Dammit it all, boy, I wish you had more of a backbone. I ain't hardly started yet. Anyway, it's getting late and we got work to do at the dock."

The young man replied, but his voice was too soft for me to make out what he said. Minutes later, I judged they left the cabin when I heard a door slam and it was quiet again.

There was a cold can of beer on the opening of my shoe. I picked it up and returned to the cot. My foot was still aching with pain. The shoe had gotten tight from my foot swelling. I wondered if I should dare try to take off the shoe, but I decided against it.

Lorelei, you have really gotten yourself into it this time, I thought. I didn't know what to do. If the older man came back he probably wouldn't hesitate to fulfill his threat. I had to think of some way to either satisfy him, or get out of the cabin before they returned. But how?

It wasn't long before the can had lost its coolness and, with my foot throbbing again, I lay back on the cot to try to rest. I had to think about what was happening.

The men must be brothers since one of them referred to "our granddaddy." The grandfather must have been on the river during the explosion and was caught in the initial surge. Given how Sharon had described the emotional climate surrounding the event, it must have been the grandfather's near drowning that tipped the scale for the brothers. "Justice must be done," the older one had said. So, just as I had suspected, the motive was revenge. It meant it was also likely one of both of them killed Adam Kincaid and chased Becky into the creek.

I was really in deep trouble if they continued to believe I had something to do with it, or even knew who did. I wondered how much time I'd have before they returned. And, what should I do while they were gone? I was exhausted, stressed, and frightened.

Chapter 16

I sat up on the cot and tested my left foot. It was still painful, and I wondered if anything had been broken. Thankfully, it had been protected by my shoe and the floor had some give to it. Otherwise, his boot would have really crushed the bones.

Okay, I thought, the only solution is to get out of here as soon as possible. I limped over to the two boarded windows at the back of the room. They were covered with cobwebs. I wrapped my hand in toilet paper, pushed the webs away, and examined the boards on the first window. I gave them a shove, but they were solidly nailed.

I looked at the objects that might serve as tools. The legs of the table or chair could be used to hammer away at the boards. Even the cot could be folded up and used as a ramrod. They would have to do.

I checked the second window. After brushing away the spider webs I found a weak board. In fact, when I pushed hard at it, the board gave way at the bottom. Someone must have pried it open to take a peek inside and decided there was nothing worth coming in for. My good luck.

I knew I had to hurry. I picked up the chair and tried simply pushing it against the boards. I was afraid to make too much noise. I didn't know how close the cabin was to where the men were working on the dock. My lack of strength and poor leverage failed to budge any of the other boards. I would have to chance making noise.

I pocketed the sandwich baggie, turned the table on its side and, with my good right foot, stomped on one of the legs to break it away from the top. It worked. Now I had something to whack the boards with. I put the chair and the overturned bucket next to the window. Holding onto the sill, I hoisted myself up and straddled both of them. I bit my lip to stifle a scream from the pain to my left foot, and leaned heavily on my right foot to keep me in balance. I slammed the boards, with all my might, using the knobby end of the table leg.

Did they hear it? I waited anxiously for any sound outside my room. There was none. Good, I thought, they might not be within earshot.

I examined the boards. Two had cracked and another budged away from the frame. I decided to go all the way with my technique and gave the boards two more solid whacks. There were now several broken and loose boards which I was able to push aside, or fully out of the window.

I peeked through the opening. The ground was about four feet below, covered with leaves, and the woods were within a few yards of the cabin. The light outside was beginning to fade. It was a good time to escape. They'd have trouble finding me in the dark.

I dropped the remaining water bottle out the window. I realized I couldn't risk simply jumping out without further injuring my foot. I took a deep breath, mentally willed a burst of adrenalin, and pushed myself out—head first. I was counting on the leaves to be deep enough to soften my fall and hoping to do a somersault landing.

Once again, I stifled a cry of pain as the injured foot landed hard on one of the boards I had knocked out. I lay on the ground stunned and gasping for breath. I knew I had to move quickly to get into the woods, and I would have to stay low to the ground. I picked up the bottled water, tucked it into the back of my slacks, and began crawling on my knees toward the tree line.

It felt like a slow excruciating journey, but soon I made it to the forest tree line. I rested for only a moment while I looked around for a stick to help support me so I could walk. I found a broken tree limb strong enough to use as a staff. I got up and, limping with pain in every step, moved deeper into the woods. My pace was steadied by the realization that, at any moment, my escape could be detected and I would be recaptured.

Finally, it grew dark enough for me to feel protected. I had no idea where I was going. It was enough to be free from captivity and the man who threatened to hurt me again.

It was obviously too dangerous for me to continue walking when I couldn't see my way. I looked around for a hiding place to spend the night. After a short time, I found what looked like a soft bed of leaves hidden by a group of cabbage palms. As I started into the palm grove, I caught a glimpse of movement out the corner of my eye. I turned to see a small deer standing stock still not far from me. It was cinnamon colored with white areas on its belly, head, and the bottom of its tail—which was standing straight up. It was a Florida white tailed deer. We stared at each other for a split second before I perceived several other deer in the darkened background. Then they all vanished into the woods, as though they had been a mirage.

I eased myself down on the patch of leaves, and devoured the sandwich the young man had given me. I was down to a half of bottle of water and knew I had to ration myself. I used a stick to dig a shallow latrine which I could use without having to travel from my hiding place. Exhausted, but satisfied I had done all I could, I gathered leaves into a heaping pile that would serve as my bed for the night. I lay down as the darkness descended and listened as the owls begin their whooing.

I wondered if it was this very spot that the deer had also planned to sleep. I scooped more leaves around my body thinking, like the deer, I might be safe from predators. The aroma of the damp earth was surprisingly pleasant. I felt like a wild creature half buried in the ground. I focused on my breathing, and slowly drifted into sleep.

My eyes blinked open with a start at hearing the crunch of footsteps nearby. I felt my heart pumping wildly with fear. I remained stock still—praying to be undetected. Could it be them, though it was barely dawn? I listened with the intense concentration of a hunted animal.

There were grunts and snorts nearby. My first thought was it might be a black bear. I had never seen one, though I knew they were in North Florida woods. I didn't even know what they sounded like. I slowly burrowed deeper into the leaves hoping whatever, or whoever it was, wouldn't see me or catch my scent. I turned my head and, through the foliage, I caught the flashing movement of a small dog-like animal. Coyote, I wondered? Was it chasing the deer I had seen last night?

Then it was quiet, except for the few early morning bird songs. I was barely breathing, and didn't relax my vigil until I was certain nothing was moving around me. As if the close animal encounter hadn't been enough to awaken me, I felt damp and itchy and needed to use the latrine. I had slept fitfully through the night; awakening at the slightest sound, trying to ignore the pain in my foot, and feeling the dewy moisture settling on my blanket of leaves. I took a carefully measured sip of water, sat up, and brushed away the leaves from around my body. I examined my arms and legs, noting the bright red mosquito bites and looking for the dreaded ticks—fortunately, none was visible.

It was time to get on the move again. I was certain, with the day light, they would soon be coming to look for me. I used the wooden stick to help me stand. My body was very stiff. It took me a few minutes to shake off the rest of the leaves and get my limbs moving.

So, where do I go now? Yesterday, I had taken a straight line leading away from the cabin. It would likely be the same path they'd take to find me. I decided to veer off at an angle to my left and move deeper into the woods. In a little while the sun would rise and I could tell my direction. Not that it would matter. I would have to walk until I encountered someone who could help me. I only hoped I would not run into any aggressive large animals—man or beast.

The heat and humidity were oppressive, and my pace was already slowed by my lame foot. I was being tortured by the constant mosquito attacks which I unsuccessfully tried to wave away with my free hand. My mouth stayed painfully dry exacerbated by the anxiety of remaining alert to every sound and movement around me.

Trudging along, I heard the clicking of cardinals and an occasional woodpecker. A large fallen tree blocked my path. I was tempted to sit and rest on its trunk until I remembered the time I was bitten by chiggers in the same way. The experience was so painful it would be intolerable added to my collection of mosquito bites.

As I moved around the fallen tree there were loud oinking sounds off to my left. Several small pigs were foraging for food in a clearing. I could just barely make out their hairy brown bodies and horse-like manes. Wild hogs, I thought, though I'd only seen photographs of them. They didn't appear at all bothered by my presence. Just to be safe, I made a wide swath around them.

The sudden sound of gunshots cracked in the air, like a bolt of lightning. I thought I'd have a heart attack. I desperately looked around for cover, and quickly ducked behind some thick shrubs. I crouched low. I was holding my breath as I wondered if the shots came from hunters, or…No, I thought, it couldn't be my kidnappers. Why would they give themselves away like that?

The shots sounded again. I heard male voices coming from the vicinity of the clearing where I had seen the pigs. The voices didn't sound like those of my captors.

"It's now, or never, Lorelei," I muttered. I got up and retraced my steps. Whoever they were, asking them for help would be better than staying lost in the woods. My throat hurt when I forced a shout, "Hello. Can you help me?"

Two men, dressed in camouflage and carrying shotguns, emerged from the brush nearby.

One of the men said, "Whoa, lady, you could get yourself shot moving around in this area. Don't you know this is hunting territory?"

"I need help," I said. "I'm lost." I know I must have sounded pitiful. And I was.

The men approached. I could see, from their appraising glances, a mixture of puzzlement and concern.

One was stockier than the other, they both looked middle aged, and had tanned faces. The one who had spoken came closer and gave me a once over before exclaiming, "What in the world? You look like you've been lost for quite awhile. What happened to you?"

His face had broad features and large kindly brown eyes topped by thick bushy brows.

"It's a long story," I said, leaning heavily on my staff. "I'm desperately thirsty. Do you have any water?"

"Here," he said, and detached a canteen from his belt, unscrewed the top and handed it to me. He noticed I was standing with my left foot slightly elevated from the ground. "Are you injured?"

I didn't respond. I drank the water in slow sips, and watched the men with what must have been a look of wary fatigue.

"Jake, put your jacket on the ground. Let's help the lady to sit down."

Jake did as suggested, and they took both my arms and helped me to the ground. They sat facing me.

"Now, tell us what happened. We'll help you."

I studied them for a moment trying to assess how much to tell them.

The one called, Jake, said, "Don't be afraid. We're just a couple of hunters after some wild pig. C'mon, how'd you get out here?"

The first hunter looked at his friend as if to say, *better go easy with her.* He smiled at me and, in a soothing voice, said, "My name is Stan. What's yours?"

"Lorelei. Lorelei Crane," I said, holding back tears of relief at finding help and at their apparent concern.

"Okay, Lorelei Crane, can you tell us what you're doing wandering alone in the woods? You look like you're pretty badly bitten up, and that foot of yours…"

"I can't tell you everything," I said. "Except that I was kidnapped and I escaped. I need to call a friend to come get me."

"Kidnapped?" The men looked at one another in amazement. "By who?"

"Look, I'm really too exhausted to go into it now," I said. "Do you have a cellphone with you? Are we near a road?"

The man called Jake shook his head, "Sorry. We don't get service in here."

"Is your car nearby? Can you take me to a sheriff's office?"

Stan got up, and said, "You sure you don't want to go a hospital first? You know, get yourself checked out and all."

"No, please. I'm okay," I said, although there was great appeal to the idea of going to a hospital where I'd have a shower, food, and treatment for my foot.

"Your call," Stan said. "Soon as we tie up our hogs we'll walk you to the truck. Do you want something to eat? I've got an energy bar in my pocket."

"Oh, that would be wonderful. Energy. Bless you. You don't know how you've saved my life." I gave him back his canteen in exchange for the energy bar which I quickly unwrapped and began eating.

Jake, who had continued sitting opposite me, looked up at his friend and exclaimed, "Ain't that something? Killed us some pigs and saved a lady's life. And the morning's hardly begun."

Both men laughed. Despite my weariness, I too, found it amusing. Rescued by kind hunters—just like Little Red Riding Hood in the Grimm fairy tale.

Chapter 17

Stan held my arm and helped me walk into the Putnam County Sheriff's Office. He stood in front of me and said to the man at the desk, "We found this woman in the woods. She says she was kidnapped and asked us to bring her here."

"Thank you," I said to Stan, as I stepped alongside him. "I can handle it now. You and your friend have been very kind."

"You want us to wait? Corroborate your story or something?"

"I don't think it'll be necessary. But I would like you to write down your full name and phone number. Jake's, too. Just in case."

Stan asked the desk clerk for paper and pen and wrote out the information. "Here," he said, handing me the paper. "You call us if you need anything. A ride back to Gainesville, whatever."

Once again, I was so moved by the man's kindness I reached up, put my one free arm around his shoulders, and gave him a big hug. "I can never thank you enough for helping me. You might have saved my life."

"Just glad we found you when we did. Those woods can be dangerous—and it's not just critters you'd need to worry about. Anyway, good luck," he said, and left.

I turned back to the clerk and asked to see a deputy. He directed me to a chair and said he'd call one.

It was still very early. The room, which looked like a doctor's waiting room, was empty except for one disheveled man who was sitting on a chair in the corner. He was leaning against the wall, sound asleep and snoring.

The heavy metal door opened. A uniformed woman, with dark short cropped hair, approached and extended her hand.

"Detective Rodriguez," she said, in an authoritative voice. Her glance took in my clothing, the collection of mosquito bites on my face and arms, and the long stick resting next to the chair. "The clerk tells me you say you've been kidnapped."

"That's right. Two hunters found me in the woods and brought me here."

"Okay. Come on back to my office. You can tell me about it." She observed my effort to get up from the chair with the use of my stick. "Do you need some help?" she asked, and reached out to help me up.

"Thank you, I can manage, unless you have a shower, some clean clothes, and can x-ray my foot."

"The shower and clothes, maybe," she said. "The x-ray you'll have to get at the hospital."

She led me through the metal door and a warren of offices until ushering me into her cubicle. She sat behind the desk and opened a notebook. I lowered myself into a metal chair. The cold office was a stark contrast to the heat of the woods. I began shivering. She noticed my discomfort and offered me a raincoat which hung on a hook near the door. I took it, thanked her and wrapped it around my shoulders.

"All right now, please spell your name for me and give me your home address and phone number."

"My name is Lorelei Crane, and..."

Her eyes opened wide, and she said, "You're Lorelei Crane? The one who was reported missing? We've been looking for you since yesterday."

She got up from her chair, and said, "Wait right here, my lieutenant will want to talk to you."

Thank you, Sharon Adelle, I thought. You must have got back safely and reported what happened.

In a few minutes, Detective Rodriguez returned with a tall, white haired officer who she introduced as Lieutenant Grayson. He sat at her desk and she brought in a chair and sat near the entrance to the small cubicle. She reached over and grabbed her notebook from the desk.

"Mrs. Crane, we've been looking for you ever since Mrs. Adelle reported your abduction. Tell us what happened. Start at the beginning. What were you doing on the river?"

I took a deep breath and envisioned the scene. "Mrs. Adelle is a friend of my ex-husband. I asked her to show me the Rodman—er, Kirkpatrick Dam. I was in South Florida when it was sabotaged and was curious about it. Anyway, we rented the canoe at a place called Pop's, and put into the river several miles below the dam. We mostly were just floating down the river, when this pontoon boat came up behind us. It was going real fast and headed straight toward our canoe."

"Can you describe the boat?"

I thought a moment. "It was white with a dark—blue, I think— awning over the front of the boat."

"Who was in the boat? What did they look like?"

"I can't really give you a description. By the time the boat was close, I saw these two men who were wearing ski masks—the kind that covers your whole head except for the eyes and mouth. Anyway, then all hell broke loose."

"What happened next?" he asked. I noticed Detective Rodriguez was making notes as I talked.

"It was all so fast. They passed us and swamped our canoe. Sharon yelled at me to try to paddle toward shore. She wanted to get out of their wake. The waves were rough. No matter how hard we tried it wasn't working."

"And then?" he probed. "What happened next?"

"The pontoon boat turned around and came back alongside us. By that time, I think I had fallen into the water, or maybe not. Maybe that's when one of them tried to grab me. It's confusing."

Detective Rodriguez looked up and asked, "If the water was so rough, how did they get close enough to the canoe to grab you?"

I thought for a moment until I remembered the hook. "They had a long pole with a hook on the end. They used it to grab the canoe and pull it toward them. Yes, I remember Sharon yelling for me to hit them with my paddle or jump—you know, to get away from them."

"And did you?"

"I think that's when one of the men had me by my blouse." I pulled at the collar where it had partially ripped away. "Before he could pull me into the boat, I lost my balance and fell in the water."

"And then?"

"I tried to swim, but I kept getting caught in the undertow of the waves. I was being pushed back toward their boat. I heard one of them yell, 'don't let her get away'. Then I saw a float board, and—well, by that time, I was just in such a panic. I wasn't thinking clearly. I grabbed the board. Of course, it was theirs and they yanked me back against their boat. I realized what was happening so I let go of the board and ducked underwater. Next thing I knew two of them were pulling me out of the water. They had me by my arms." I rubbed my arms remembering how much it hurt to be jerked up that way.

"What was Mrs. Adelle doing during this time?"

"I'm not sure, but I think the canoe had turned over and she was in the water. I heard her yelling something as the boat pulled away."

Detective Rodriguez interjected, "She told us she was yelling for you not to worry. That she'd get help."

The lieutenant continued, "So now you're on their boat. You were close to them. Did you get to see what the men looked like?"

"I'm afraid not. As soon as they pulled me onto to the boat, they slammed me face down on the deck. One of them got a knee in my back, and tied my hands and legs behind me. When he turned me over, he was still wearing a ski mask. All I could see were his bloodshot eyes and puffy red lips. He smelled like beer. Finally, he put a blindfold over my eyes and stuffed a cloth in my mouth. I must have passed out, or they injected me with something, because the next thing I knew I was in this old cabin."

"When you were being tied, did either one say anything to you? Anything you remember?"

"After the rag was stuffed in my mouth, I started gagging. Beer breath told me to breathe through my nose. It was helpful, actually."

Lt. Grayson looked at the detective and said, "Let's give Mrs. Crane a break. She's been through a lot. Is there anything we can get for you? Coffee or something to eat?"

Rodriguez said, "She asked for a shower and clean clothes. I think she's about my size. I've got some extra clothes in my locker."

"Sure, let her get cleaned up and meet back here in a half hour. All right with you, Mrs. Crane?"

"Oh, yes," I said. "Thank you."

The shower felt absolutely wonderful—even with my shoes on. I was afraid to take off the left shoe which had expanded to accommodate my foot. The pain had become a bearable dull throbbing sensation. Detective Rodriguez generously loaned me a pair of wide bottomed jeans and a blouse, as well as a comb and lipstick. I almost felt normal, except the itchy bites all over my body.

We went back into her office, and she brought me a cup of coffee and a donut. In a few minutes, Lt.Grayson returned.

"Feeling better?" he asked, and gave me a sympathetic look. "You certainly look a lot better."

"Yes, thank you, Lieutenant. Detective Rodriguez was very generous to loan me her clothes."

"Okay, so let's resume where we left off. After the boat ride, you found yourself in a cabin. Can you describe it?"

I described the cabin, and he asked if I ever got a look at the kidnappers.

I replied, "I never saw their faces. I woke up to hammering on the outside of the door. It sounded like they were fixing a lock. Then, a man came into the room and was still wearing the ski mask. I guess he was about five foot nine, youngish, slim, and dressed in jeans and a black T-shirt with X-Men written across it. He had a limp."

He studied me for a moment, and said, "You have a remarkable memory for someone in such a traumatic situation." There was a touch of skepticism in his tone.

"I'm an actress. It's my job is to pay attention to details, voices and other nuances."

The lieutenant nodded—apparently satisfied by my explanation. He continued with his questions. The detective kept writing and didn't look up from her notebook.

"So you did have contact with the other man?"

"Oh, yes," I said, pointing to my foot. "I had contact all right. He was an older guy—beer breath. The one who stomped on my foot when he didn't like my answers to his questions. The young one had tied my hands to the chair and blindfolded me before he came into the room. When I screamed, the young guy called out to protest and was told to shut up. 'J.T.' was the name he called."

At the mention of the name, Lieutenant Grayson glanced at Detective Rodriguez, as if to make sure she got it in her notes.

"What did this J.T. ask you?"

I proceeded to tell them about Earth Save and the questions about members he believed were responsible for bombing the dam. I said he thought I was one of them, or at least knew who they were. The older man made reference to their grandfather who was almost drowned because of the dam burst. I mentioned that the young man was less aggressive and seemed intimidated by the older one. I assumed they were brothers since the phrase "our granddaddy" was used by the older man.

"Let me get this straight," the lieutenant said, and he leaned forward. He gave me an intense look. "You never saw their faces, but you're certain you heard the younger man call his partner by the initials 'J.T.' and make reference to their grandfather."

"Yes, I'm certain."

"Would you recognize their voices if you heard them again?"

"As I said, I have a memory for voices. I also remembered J.T.'s exact words, 'Justice must be done.' It was chilling because…"

I didn't get to finish my sentence before the lieutenant stood up, said he'd be back, and motioned Detective Rodriguez to follow him.

I sat there for what seemed like a half hour before Rodriguez returned. She said, "Sorry for the interruption, but we think we might know the identity of your captors."

"You do? Who are they?"

"Afraid I can't tell you. But be assured they're going to be taken into custody very soon. In the meantime, Lt. Grayson asked me to take down the rest of your story. How you escaped and met the men who brought you into our office this morning. I'd like to get their names and contact information, as well."

I recounted my escape from the cabin. I described how I had managed to break out of the boarded window and make my way into the woods where I spent the night. I left out the somewhat picturesque details of my animal encounters.

When I finished my story, Detective Rodriguez raised her head, from the notebook in which she had been writing, and gave me a look of admiration.

"That was very brave of you. And, with that foot of yours, it's amazing you were able to get away and hide so well."

"I didn't feel brave," I replied. "I felt more desperate than at any time in my life. I was certain J.T. would do something worse to me if I had remained in the cabin. In fact, I have a hunch that J.T. and his brother may have committed a crime in Gainesville."

"What crime?" Rodriguez asked, holding her pen above the notebook.

"It's a long story," I said, and immediately regretted mentioning it. I was so weary. It had just slipped out. I knew if they checked with the Alachua County Sheriff's Office, or GPD, they'd learn the Kincaid case had been closed.

She continued looking at me, waiting for an explanation.

"Sorry, don't pay attention to what I said. I'm still pretty confused. I really need to have my foot looked at. It's hurting pretty badly again. Any chance of getting to the hospital?" I wanted to distract the her from my earlier blunder. Fortunately, she was very sympathetic.

"Of course, I'm sorry we've kept you so long," she said. "But I know we'll want to interview you again. Let me arrange for transport. In the meantime, would you like to use my phone to call anyone? I'm sure you have family and friends who are worried about you."

I thought about Sharon Adelle who must have been terribly upset by what happened and would want to know I was safe. Also, I had left my handbag with my car keys and cell phone in her car. Then I remembered Delcie. We had a dinner date for Monday night. She would be worried when she couldn't reach me. Before I could think about who first to call and how to get their numbers, Lieutenant Grayson reappeared.

"Do you know a Detective McBride from Alachua County Sheriff's Office?"

"Yes, I do. He's a good friend." I felt a wave of relief just hearing Homer's name.

143

The lieutenant gave me an amused look. "Well, he must be a very good friend. He's been checking with our office every few hours to see if we've found you. In fact, he asked permission to come over this morning and help us with the case. You might want to give him a call before we take you over to the hospital."

Chapter 18

Homer and Delcie were in the hospital waiting area after my foot had been x-rayed and treated. I limped toward them on a pair of crutches. They were harder to use than my long stick. I let them throw it away along with the shoe they cut off of my swollen foot.

Delcie immediately rushed over and gave me a big hug. "We've been so worried about you."

Homer stood by, glaring at me. He said, "You just can't let the law do their job, can you? Lieutenant Grayson told me some of what you've been through. From what I heard, you're lucky you're only on crutches."

"How's your foot? What'd the doctor say?" Delcie asked, casting a disapproving glance at Homer.

"Oh, my big toe is broken, I have a small hematoma under the nail and the rest of my foot is just bruised. I was relieved to hear there wasn't more damage. It was so painful; it felt like my foot had been mangled by a truck running over it. Anyway, they put a splint on the toe, gave me some painkillers and told me how to take care of it at home. I'll have my doctor in Gainesville check it in a week or so."

I looked at Homer. "How did you get in on this? Lieutenant Grayson told me you even volunteered for the search."

"I'll tell you about it on the way back to Gainesville."

"What about my car? Sharon Adelle has my handbag with the keys."

"Not to worry," Delcie said. "The detective gave us her name and number. We stopped by there and got your stuff. I'm going to drive your car back to Gainesville. She wants you to call her as soon as you're able. Nice lady."

They flanked me protectively as we left the hospital. Homer's car was standing at the curb. Before he helped me into it, I thanked

Delcie. "I'm so glad to see you. You'll bring my bag up to the condo when we get back to town, won't you?"

"Of course," she said. "Do you want me to pick up anything—medication, food?"

"No, dear. I've got everything I need—especially with the two of you as my best friends." My eyes filled with tears in a surge of emotion at seeing them. Their presence was reassuring. It made me feel everything was going to be all right.

Delcie, responding to my emotions, put an arm around me and kissed me on the cheek. Homer muttered something, opened the car door, took my crutches, and helped me inside. He put the crutches in the trunk and we left.

We started driving out of Palatka. Instead of asking me questions, or lecturing me, as I had expected him to do, he was unusually silent.

"Homer, I can't thank you enough for being there for me. How did you find out?"

He said, "Delcie called when she wasn't able to locate you for dinner. At least we knew where to start looking for you."

"I'm so glad I thought to leave her a message about my trip to Palatka."

"Lorelei, I know you're a risk taker, but this time I was really afraid for you. While we drove over to the hospital, I talked with Lt.Grayson. He told me, in confidence, one of the men they believe responsible—J.T.Tyler—has been in trouble ever since he returned from Iraq. He's had a lot of mental problems, and his violent temper is widely known. They've picked him up for assault a few times, but nobody would press charges. He comes from a very close-knit old Putnam County family."

"That's interesting, and it certainly explains a lot. Did you learn anything about the younger brother? The other kidnapper?"

"Uh huh. Grayson told me Danny Tyler's enrolled at the local college. Believe it or not—his major is Criminal Justice. Apparently he's a good kid, who idolizes his older brother, and pretty much tags along with him. Oh, and their grandfather is well known in the community. He's been raising hell around town about nearly drowning when the dam was blown."

"No wonder they knew right away who was responsible for my kidnapping. Anyway, Homer, I am truly sorry to have caused you and Delcie such alarm. All I intended to do was see the dam and learn more about what's happened since it was breached."

McBride snickered and gave me a sideways glance. "Lorelei Crane, I know you better than that. You were going to snoop around Palatka to prove your theory that some locals were taking revenge on Earth Save members. Tell the truth—isn't that really what you were up to?"

"Well, with you off the case, and that Sherlock Holmes fellow deciding Kincaid's murder had to do with drugs..."

"His name is Kyle Watson," Homer corrected. "Look, Lorelei, contrary to the way you sometimes act, you are not a detective. Yes, I have complimented some of your investigative skills in the past, but..."

"My dear Detective McBride, a man was murdered, and whatever else you may say about Adam Kincaid he did serve his country in war. And what about my friend Becky? She's been severely traumatized, and it's likely by the same people who've frightened other members of Earth Save. None of this has yet been fully investigated," I said, with passion. I remembered J.T.'s assertion, "Justice must be served."

Homer took a hand off the wheel, and held it up in a half-hearted surrender. "Okay, I get your point. What would you like me to do about it? Did you hear the men who abducted you make any confession about Kincaid, or the Haimovitz girl?"

"No, not exactly, but I learned they had more than one motive for revenge."

"Which was?"

"It wasn't simply breaching the dam, but the older brother also mentioned what happened to their grandfather. Furthermore, I recognized a man, working at the Palatka canoe outfitters, who was at Charley's the night I met Jeffrey for the Earth Save meeting. He paid an unusual amount of attention to me. I've learned his name is

147

Lonnie. He's been hanging around the Charley's for awhile. I think he must be the one who gave J.T. the names of Earth Save members. The ones who they decided were responsible for the Rodman."

"All circumstantial," Homer said.

"If the brothers went so far as to kidnap me, don't you think they also could have been involved in a more serious crime?"

Homer didn't respond. He appeared to be considering what I said, and I wanted to give him a chance to reflect upon it. I shifted my weight closer to the passenger door, and looked out of the window as we drove along the road to Gainesville.

"Do you like this new four lane road?" I asked, breaking the silence.

"Yes, it's quicker and safer," he replied.

"I liked the old one better. It felt more like you were driving in the country."

We passed the intersection, at the town of Interlachen, and I said, "See what I mean—look at that pretty lake. The drive is so much more interesting on this part of the road."

"Okay, Lorelei. You can stop the travelogue. I understand why you continue to believe there's more to the Kincaid case and your friend's disappearance. I tried to suggest that to Watson when he took over. You have to understand, he's got a very heavy caseload—mine on top of what he already had—so naturally he was eager to close the case as soon as possible. Realistically, the evidence for a bad drug deal was a lot more substantial than anything else they had."

"And what about justice?" I asked.

He gave me a look as though to say, "Are you kidding?"

"I just can't let it go. Kincaid's dead, but Becky and her family need some explanation as to what happened to her. And there are others whose lives have been seriously disrupted, as well." I was thinking about Bear and Tim Grantly—both of whom seemed to have fled Gainesville. "I think Tyler has the answers."

"And, just how do you propose to get it out of him?" asked McBride.

"I don't know yet, but I'll think of something." The something I thought of was really someone—Danny Tyler, J.T.'s young brother. I didn't know exactly how, but I felt sure I could persuade him to provide information about the Gainesville incidents.

"You'd have to visit him in jail to get it. Once you ID the men, and the detectives gather evidence, the two of them are going to be facing some serious prison time."

We reached the outskirts of Gainesville, and I felt grateful to be back home. I had only been gone for a day and a half, but it seemed longer. Funny how your perception of time is. Sometimes it passes quickly, and at other times—like my last 24 hours—it feels stretched out far beyond its actual duration. Must be something in Einstein's theories about that.

In about ten minutes, we pulled up to the entrance to my condo. Homer retrieved the crutches from the trunk, and helped me out of the car.

He said, "Sorry to leave you here, Lorelei, but I've got to get back to the office. Delcie should be along at any minute, and can help you with whatever you need. I'll call you later." He gave me a perfunctory peck on the cheek.

I thanked him again, and hobbled into the lobby of my building. I was bone weary, and decided to wait there for Delcie. She had the keys to my condo and could help me get settled.

"Lorelei, you have pulled some damn crazy stunts, but this idea of yours beats all."

Delcie was sitting in the arm chair across from me, and sipping a glass of Pinot. I was stretched out on the sofa, in my most comfortable loungewear, with my left foot elevated by several couch cushions. The remains of our lunch were on the coffee table. It was a tuna salad which Delcie thoughtfully prepared while I was changing clothes,

"It's not so crazy. Remember *In Cold Blood?* Truman Capote did the same thing, and he eventually got his story."

"You are not Capote. Why would Danny Tyler make a confession to you if it gets his brother charged with murder?"

"Because he's basically a good guy—I don't think he's capable of violence. He yelled at his brother to stop assaulting me."

"Yeah, he yelled. Did he actually stop him from doing it? And, if the kid wasn't directly responsible for Kincaid's death, he probably went along with it—maybe even helped. At the least, he'd be an accessory to the crime—and that's a felony."

"I'm sure he wasn't directly involved. I mean, Delcie, the boy gave me a peanut butter and jelly sandwich—probably his own lunch—and he has a limp. How bad could he be? Besides, I'm sure I can make him like me."

"I'm sure you can, Lorelei. You'll be acting like his own dear departed mother."

"Did they tell you his mother is dead?" I asked.

"No, you what I mean. Okay, so the younger brother is a sweet, nonviolent guy with a limp—whatever that has to do with anything. Look at it from this perspective, even if your idea could work, do you really want to spend your time in the Putnam County jail trying to break him down? I thought your rehearsals were cranking up for the opening. Isn't it in a few weeks?"

"Yes, of course, I'm going to be busier than ever getting ready for the opening. What I find interesting, is that both you and Homer—a law enforcement officer and a former one—seem so disinterested in seeking justice for Kincaid, Becky, and the others."

Delcie waved a hand protesting my conclusion. "Just a minute there, girlfriend. Speaking for myself, it's not for want of interest. Of course, I'd like to see the redneck bastard get his due. It's just not your job to do it. When you meet with the Putnam Sheriff's Office again, to ID the two men, you should tell them why you believe this Tyler guy might be responsible for a murder in Gainesville. Persuade them to investigate. That's the sensible thing to do. Not go rushing off, like some Miss Marple, trying to expose the killer by getting his brother to rat out on him."

I didn't respond. I knew she was right. It was a hair-brained idea to think I could get a confession from Danny Tyler. Yet, if I didn't give it a try, I would forever wonder if crazy J.T. would terrorize someone else. As for Becky, didn't she deserve to know that her pursuers were prosecuted?

Delcie looked at her watch, and put her wine glass down on the table. "I've got to go, Lor. So, what are you going to do?"

"Guess, I'll visit the jail and bring some cookies to Danny Tyler."

"Shut up," Delcie said, grinning. "Guess that's why I love you so much. You just don't think anything about stickin' your hand in the bushes where you just saw a snake."

I laughed at her comment, especially considering my morbid fear of snakes.

"Okay," she said, heading for the door. "But please let me know when you're going over there. Hopefully, J.T.'s the only psycho in his family. I don't want anybody else tryin' to harm my best friend."

"I will, Delcie. I promise."

After she left, I stayed on the couch and dosed off. I awoke to the sound of my cell phone on the table next to me. The light in the living room had dimmed. I guessed I'd slept through the afternoon and into the early evening. It was a missed call from Homer. I sat up and called him back.

"How are you doing?" he asked. "Do you need anything?"

"No, I'm fine. Delcie helped me get settled. I guess I've slept all afternoon."

"That's good. You needed rest. I've got some news for you."

"What's that?"

"I talked with Detective Watson today, and told him everything you told me on the way back to town."

"Yes, and...?"

"He's interested in your theory. He'd like to talk with you when you're up to it."

"Oh, Homer, that's wonderful. Thank you so much. I knew you'd do the right thing."

"Well, I think you did make a case for reopening the investigation. Let me know when you're going to see Watson."

The cell phone rang again just after I ended my conversation with Homer. It was Jeremy.

"How are you doing?" he asked. "Rick said you had some kind of an accident and broke your toe. What happened?"

"It's a long story, but I'm taking medication and keeping my foot elevated. That's why I couldn't come to rehearsal today."

"Rotten luck," he said. "We...I missed you. Will you be coming tomorrow?"

"Oh yes, I plan to. I'm on crutches, but it's my left foot so I can drive."

"I can pick you up if you like."

"No, Jeremy, that's sweet of you, but it isn't necessary."

"Well then, I'll see you tomorrow."

"Yes, tomorrow," I said, feeling drowsy again.

There was a pause. Instead of saying goodbye, as I expected, Jeremy said, "Uh, Lorelei, I wonder if we could get together after rehearsal tomorrow—at your place. There's something I want to tell you."

I became alert to the hesitancy in his voice. "Really? What is it?"

"It needs telling in person. How about it? I've got a good Beaujolais I've been saving. I can bring it along."

My curiosity won out. I agreed to the meeting, and we said goodbye.

Chapter 19

I felt refreshed after a good night's sleep. I had a light breakfast and made several phone calls. First, I called my doctor and made an appointment to have my toe examined. Next, I spoke with my mother at the ALF in South Florida—I didn't tell her about my so-called accident. I tried calling Sharon Adelle, but she didn't answer so I left a voice message. I saved my last call for Detective Watson at Gainesville Police Department. It sounded like he was in a hurry. He said he could see me today if I got over there before noon.

On my way out of the condo, I received a call from Detective Rodriguez in Palatka.

"Mrs. Crane, how are you doing? How did things go at the hospital?"

"I'm fine thanks," I said. "It was a broken toe—not my whole foot. It's still painful, and I'm going to see my doctor tomorrow. I can't seem to get used to the crutches."

"I know what you mean. Anyway, I'm glad it wasn't more serious. The reason I'm calling is to ask you to come in to identify two men we suspect to be your kidnappers."

"That's great. Can it wait until tomorrow? I've got an appointment with the Gainesville Police Department in just a little while, and I have to be at rehearsals this afternoon."

"Okay, we can schedule it for first thing tomorrow. Can you be here by ten o'clock?"

"I'll be there. Oh, and I'll bring your clothes back to you."

The conversation ended by my telling her how much I appreciated everything she did for me. I remembered there was a 24 hour cleaners, on my way to the police department, where I could drop off her clothes, and pick them up tomorrow before going Palatka.

Driving out on University Avenue, I reflected on the appointment tomorrow in Putnam County, as well as the meeting I was going to with GPD's Detective Watson. I felt a surge of excitement at how fast things were finally moving toward resolution of the Kincaid mystery and Becky's disappearance.

Detective Watson came out shortly after I arrived at GPD. He was a balding thirty something man, about average height and weight, wearing chinos and a maroon polo shirt. He looked harried, and his shoulders hunched as he quickly led me to his office.

After we were seated, Watson opened a file on his desk and quickly scanned its contents. His face had a pleasant roundness to it and, except for his continual frown; he could have been type cast as the friendly boy next door.

Finally, he looked up, and said, "So, Mrs. Crane, Detective McBride thinks you have information that might lead us to reopen the Kincaid case. Please tell me how you first became involved in this matter, and what you've learned about it?"

It took me a minute or so to mentally compose the sequence of events that started me on my investigative quest.

"It began a little over a month ago. I first learned of Adam Kincaid's death after I returned to Gainesville from a long stay in South Florida. Friends were concerned about the investigation and wanted to know how it was proceeding. Adam was their friend."

"And a member of the Earth Save activist group," he added, after glancing down at his folder.

"Yes. One of them, Becky Haimovitz, seemed especially fearful as a result of his death. She asked if I could find out anything about it since I knew Detective McBride."

"He told me you provided some help to him during two of his murder investigations."

Is that all he said about me, I wondered, feeling slighted—I provided some help?

I went on. "Naturally, since he was involved in the case, he told me he couldn't provide any detailed information." I didn't mention his not telling me, until yesterday, about the drug evidence they'd found at Kincaid's apartment. Homer was a sly one, I thought.

"That's correct. At the time it was still an ongoing investigation."

"What he did tell me, however, made me afraid for my friends."

"And that was what exactly?"

"Well, he related the recent murder of a High Springs activist and of a Marion County environmentally oriented commissioner who had gotten death threats. It made me worry there might even be some plot against environmentalists that would endanger my friends."

Watson flashed a crooked smile, as though he found the notion amusing.

"He also mentioned that Earth Save members had been interviewed in an attempt to find a motive for Kincaid's death, but that everyone was pretty tight-lipped. He said the investigation was proceeding slowly. At that point, I volunteered to try and get information from the members since…"

"You're connected with their leader." He looked down at the file. "Jeffrey Waterman."

"He's my first husband. Anyway, Jeffrey agreed to let me to attend an Earth Save meeting. They're pretty secretive, but I think they accepted me because of him."

"I can understand their secrecy and lack of cooperation with our office. In the past, they've engaged in illegal activities, and we've arrested a number of them," he said. There was a hostile edge to his voice.

I ignored his comment. "At the end of the meeting, we realized that Becky Haimovitz wasn't there. It was totally unlike her not to show up. We went looking for her and couldn't find her. Of course, she did show up after a few days, but she'd been seriously traumatized by whatever happened to her."

"It says here that you and Delcie Wright reported her missing after finding her automobile at a friend's house. Is that correct?"

"Yes, the car door was wide open, and her handbag and its contents were strewn around. It looked to us as though she had been either abducted, or just escaped to somewhere. It was extremely suspicious, to say the least."

He turned a page in the folder, and said, "Our report says she showed up a few days later, at the Farmers Market, and was taken home by her parents. There haven't been reports of any more incidents of that nature. Now, let's talk about the past few days. What were you doing in Putnam County? Detective McBride told me you were a victim of a kidnapping."

"That's right, I was. I recently learned that, while I was in South Florida, the Rodman Dam had been blown up. I didn't hear about it earlier because I was preoccupied with a lot of personal and professional matters. Anyway, I went to Palatka to see for myself what it looked like. A friend of Jeffrey's offered to take me out on the river, and that's when I was kidnapped."

"Yes, I heard you were kidnapped while you were on the river," Watson said. "Tell me about it. And try to give me as much detail as you can."

I proceeded to describe my kidnapping, the cabin, how I escaped, and was rescued by the two hunters. I told him I was going to Palatka tomorrow to identify the two men who might have been my kidnappers.

When I had finished my story, he said, "You've had quite an experience, Mrs. Crane. I admire your courage and your resourcefulness."

"Thank you," I replied, feeling a bit smug thinking I had done Homer a service in proving, to his colleague, that I wasn't just some pretty actress McBride had taken a fancy to.

"I'm told you believe the kidnappers are the same men involved in the Kincaid case, as well as your friend's disappearance."

"I am, but I can't prove it. I was going to try to get the younger man, Danny Tyler, to tell me what he knew about it. I thought I could gain his confidence, and…"

For the first time, Detective Watson's face relaxed into a genuine smile. "Look, Mrs. Crane, Detective McBride thinks very highly of you, but this is our job. I'll tell you right now, I'm interested in the man at the canoe outfitters. The one who you believe to be the same person you saw at Charley's bar. I'm also interested in Joshua Tyler's remark to you about seeking justice for the incident with his grandfather. You've given me a new and interesting perspective on the Kincaid case."

"Oh, I'm so glad."

He looked at his watch, and his face crumpled into a frown once again. "I've got to end our conversation now. Please be assured, I will contact the Putnam Sheriff's Office and follow the investigation of your kidnapping. I'm also going to have the Charley's bartender re-interviewed about his patrons. The man you mentioned—Lonnie was his name—has not been questioned by us. He might have information about the night Mr. Kincaid left the bar and was later found murdered."

He stood up, I lifted myself onto my crutches, and we were both ready to leave.

"Thank you for your time, Mrs. Crane. I'll let Detective McBride know about our conversation."

Everyone at the theater was very solicitous when I appeared in the rehearsal hall on crutches. My fellow actors were eager to learn how I had broken my toe. I told them I had been injured in a kidnapping. The flat statement evoked the expected reaction—expressions of disbelief, hands over mouths in shock, and eyes widened in surprise. Jeremy immediately came to my side with a look of alarm. Although I'd be embarrassed to admit it to them, the actress in me relished every second of the dramatic impact which accompanied my explanation. Rick joined the group just as one of the actors was asking where the kidnapping had occurred. Others followed, demanding details. Acknowledging Rick's presence, I said the story was too long to tell before rehearsals began. I promised to relate it to them during the break.

In his characteristically droll voice, Rick said, "Okay, so Lorelei was kidnapped. Now, let's get back to the barber shop—Todd is getting ready to off his competitor, and Mrs. Lovett's pies are about to be selling like hot cakes. I want you to split up and rehearse your lines and blocking. As I told you yesterday, when we altered the schedule, we're starting with Act I, Scene 5. Renee will here in a little while."

157

"Are you all right?" Jeremy whispered, as our group was getting settled with their revised scripts and blocking notes.

"Yes, Jeremy, I'm fine. It was a traumatic experience, but you'll hear about it later."

"Are we still on for tonight?"

"I don't see why not."

In about a half an hour, Renee appeared and we began to rehearse. Fortunately, I had only to stand in one place for Mrs. Lovett's few lines. After exiting the scene, I was able to sit down and enjoy watching the other actors. They had all improved since last week. I was especially impressed by Jeremy's nuanced performance as Todd. At the end of the scene, Todd strangles Alfredo, shoves him into a trunk, and has a wickedly satirical interaction with the servant, Tobias. When Tobias leaves, Todd slits Alfredo's throat, and breaks into a soliloquy on death. I was enthralled—ghoul that I am.

A break was called around five. Drinks and sandwiches had been delivered. Everyone gathered around me. They expected I would tell them about my kidnapping. Which I did. There were many questions. Some of them I answered honestly, and to some I responded, "I don't know." I didn't think it wise to reveal everything.

Rick showed up with a metal walker. "Here," he said. "We had it down in props. My mother broke her ankle, and couldn't manage the crutches. The walker was easier."

I tried it, and found he was right. It was much easier to manage than the crutches.

Before the break ended, Renee called me aside.

"I don't know what you've been into that got you kidnapped, but I don't like it one bit."

"I'm fine now, Renee," I said, taking her comment for one of sympathy. "I believe they've identified the men who kidnapped me. And, hopefully, I may only need this walker for a short time. I'm going to the doctor tomorrow." I thought I was allaying her concern about my well being. Instead, her response caught me by complete surprise.

"I know you believe you're okay. My concern is that our show will be opening in a few short weeks. What if you still need the walker by then? Not to mention that whatever you were involved with may put you in jeopardy again, or something else might happen. My intuition tells me not to take the chance counting on you during this run. "

I started to speak, but she continued, "I don't even want to know what you've been doing. My sole concern is that you're able to be at each and every rehearsal, and that by our opening you won't need that thing," she said, looking with disdain at the aluminum walker. "So, I've decided to have Cassie Woodruff understudy you. If it's necessary, her part as Johanna will be easier to fill at the last minute."

"Really, Renee, I promise you there's no need to do that. I'm…"

"It's settled, Lorelei. Nothing personal. You know I adore you. Besides, think of it this way, Cassie deserves a chance at an adult role, don't you agree?"

"Yes, you're right. And I do apologize for causing all of this trouble."

I didn't get to talk with Cassie before rehearsals resumed, but I could tell from her looks that Renee had already discussed it with her. Cassie was my friend. If being my understudy meant giving her a professional stretch, I was fine with it.

We finished rehearsing around nine thirty. Jeremy helped me out to my car. We agreed to meet back at my condo in a half an hour. On the way home, I tried guessing what it was he wanted to tell me. He said it was something that required us to meet in private. My curiosity peaked. My toe throbbed.

At ten o'clock sharp, the doorbell sounded, and I ushered him in. He showed me the bottle of Beaujolais he'd brought with him.

"Please open it yourself. The opener is on the kitchen counter, wine glasses are right above it. Fix yourself a glass. I'm still on pain meds, so just bring me a glass of water." Jeremy nodded and went into the kitchen.

I tuned the radio to the smooth jazz station, and settled myself on the couch in the living room. I was eager to hear his news.

He returned from the kitchen with a small tray on which he had the wine bottle, his glass and my water."

"Here you are m'dam," he said, and with a mock bow, handed me the water glass.

"Jeremy, you were superb today," I said. "You must really have been doing a lot of home work, because you had me totally captivated by the emotion you brought to the scene."

Jeremy, who had settled at the other end of the couch, was apparently so emboldened by my compliment that he moved right next to me. "Thank you, Lorelei. Coming from you, that's high praise. Too bad Renee didn't like it as much as you did. You know she gave me a note on the speech in Scene 5 after I cut Alfredo's throat? 'This isn't Hamlet,' she said."

"Pish tosh, you don't have to accept everything she says. I was the audience, and I found it entirely engaging. It is a bit Shakespearean, and was not one bit over-acted."

"I'm relieved you didn't think so." Jeremy said. "By the way, how's the foot?"

"Toe," I corrected. "It doesn't hurt too much thanks to the pills I'm taking." And then I told him about my meeting with Renee.

"Well, I can see her point, but..." He took a sip of wine. "Sorry you're missing this, it's quite delicious."

I yawned. It was embarrassing, but uncontrollable. "Excuse me, but I've just had an exhausting few days. I can't wait any longer, Jeremy, what was it you wanted to tell me?"

"Maybe this isn't the right time," he said.

"No, please. I've been curious ever since you mentioned it. I promise I won't yawn in your face again."

He put his wine glass on the table, and took the glass of water from my hand. He turned, put his arms around me, and gave me a passionate kiss. It was a prolonged embrace, mainly because I was so taken aback by it I didn't push him away.

He finally let me go, and I caught my breath.

"Jeremy, where in the world is that coming from? You told me you were gay."

He leaned back, and with a rueful smile, said, "That's what I wanted you to think, but I'm not gay."

"But," I sputtered. "At the restaurant, you were so convincing. I believed you."

"That night, I was completely caught off-guard by you…by your obvious attraction to me. Before I could think about it, I defaulted into my usual defense."

"Defense? But why?"

"Look, Lorelei, I know I'm an attractive man, and I certainly enjoy the attention I get from women, but it can also be more than just a nuisance. So, from time to time, I let on that I'm gay."

"That seems rather extreme."

"I know it appears that way, but a few years ago I was stalked by a young actress. It got to be quite serious. She showed up everywhere I went. Then one night, when I came home from the theater, I found her waiting for me in my apartment—in the bedroom. I don't know how she managed to get in. Anyway, when I rebuffed her she became quite violent. Finally, I made up this story about being gay, and she eventually calmed down and left. It's what gave me the idea to use the line whenever I feel someone is coming on to me, and I don't want the attention. Some women pretend to be married for the same reason."

"I'm sure what happened to you was an awful experience, but if you didn't want my attention, as you put it, what's changed?"

"I've come to realize I really am beginning to have feelings for you, Lorelei. I surprised myself by how worried I was when they said you had an accident."

My jaw must have dropped, because he gently placed a finger under my chin. He moved back a little, and stared at me with a bemused look on his face.

I said, "Jeremy Hastings, you are some accomplished actor, aren't you?"

"Guilty as charged," he said. "So what do you think? Do we have a chance for romance?"

Chapter 20

Delcie offered to drive me to Palatka to identify the Tyler brothers. On the way, I told her about my surprising encounter with Jeremy Hastings the previous evening.

"He sounds like a pretty cool dude. Did you hook up with him?" She cast a wicked look in my direction.

"'Hook up' is that what they're calling it now?"

"That's what my student interns call it. Did you, or did you not sleep with him last night?"

"No, I didn't. Really, Delcie, you must think…"

"Just asking. I could use some vicarious romance."

"Romance? To begin with there was the slight fact of my broken toe that still had to be elevated and iced. In any event, I acted non-committal, and got him out the door before he could think about making serious moves on me. Truth is, I'm still trying to figure out what he's up to. When he first told me he was gay, it felt authentic."

"You think he's playing on both teams?"

"My, aren't you the slangy one today. To answer your question, it's possible. Not that it would matter all that much to me. Yes, on second thought, I think it would."

"What about McBride? Anything going on with him? I was surprised how worried he was when I called to tell him you'd gone missing. And you seemed awfully glad to see him at the hospital."

"Let's not even waste our time speculating about Homer McBride. I think at this point we're just friends. But now that you've grilled me about my personal relationships, how about you? I haven't heard you mention a man in your life since…what his name?"

"Exactly, I never was good at history either. Anyway, the only men in my life right now are paying for my services—clients. I may be taking a vow of chastity, but I'm not into poverty."

162

We continued talking about family and the theater all the way into Palatka. Delcie knew where she was going, and soon we parked outside the Putnam County Sheriff's Office.

Detective Rodriguez came out to meet me. I handed her the bag of clothes from the cleaners, and thanked her again for the loan. She led me into a windowless room where there were a couple of chairs facing a flat screened TV monitor.

"We asked both the men in to answer some questions," she said.

"And they agreed? Why would they do that if they didn't have to?"

"It would look suspicious if they refused to cooperate. Take a look, and listen carefully. Let me know what you think."

I watched as Joshua Tyler, aka J.T.. was led into a ten by ten room which contained a table with two nondescript devices on it. There were two chairs on either side of the table. Otherwise, the room was bare. The video and the audio reception were so clear and sharp it was as though I was in the room with them. I immediately recognized his voice.

I said, "That's definitely him—the one who broke my toe. I have a keen ear for voices, and I'd recognize his anywhere."

"Listen some more. We want you to be very positive about the voices, and anything else that identifies them. Especially since you didn't actually see their faces."

I listened and watched as the interrogation proceeded with some general questions. Finally, he was asked if he'd heard about the kidnapping on the Ocklawaha. He said he may have heard about on the news. When asked where he was yesterday afternoon, J.T. responded that he was home all day with his brother. He gave only short answers to other questions.

I studied my abductor as an actor appraises a character in a play, or film. His appearance alone cast him in the role of the derelict. He was unshaven, his hair looked dirty and uncombed. He had the same puffy red lips and bloodshot eyes I remembered seeing when he landed me on the boat. His face looked bloated, whether from drink or drugs, I could only guess. He was wearing camouflage pants and a washed-out green T-shirt. As for his demeanor, instead of appearing aggressive—as he had been with me—he gave the impression of someone who was depressed and distant.

After a long pause in the questioning, his interrogator said, "I understand your grandfather was on the river when the dam burst."

Suddenly, J.T. reacted as though he'd been stuck with a cattle prod. His body stiffened, and he gave the detective an angry look. "He was very nearly drowned. They almost got my little nephew, too. They was out together, fishing on the river."

There was another pause before the detective continued, "I can understand why you'd be pretty angry about that. Do you know the names of any of the people who were responsible?"

Now J.T. appeared sly, and said, "I don't know names, just it was them damn Gainesville terrorists. The ones blew up the dam." He glanced at the door and asked, "When can I get out of here. You gonna arrest me for something? Do I need a lawyer?"

The detective ignored his questions, and shifted topics by asking about fishing in the reservoir. J.T. seemed to relax as they shared experiences fishing for bass. The detective finally asked if J.T. owned a pontoon boat. He denied owning one, and began to appear restless. The interview concluded, and the detective led him out of the room.

After a few minutes, the younger brother was brought in. The same detective began his questioning in much the same fashion as before.

"Oh, Jesus, how dumb," I said.

Detective Rodriguez asked, "What?"

"The younger one, Danny, is wearing the same X-Men T-shirt and jeans he wore when they kidnapped me. I recognize his body build and his voice."

"Are you certain," she asked.

"Absolutely. That's him. I got a good look at him in the cabin. Did you notice the slight limp when he walked in?"

"I did. That's pretty convincing," Rodriguez said. "Wait here. I'm going to talk with my Lieutenant. I'll be right back."

Detective Rodriguez left the room, and I remained fascinated watching the conduct of the interview. I studied the expression on Danny's face as he professed ignorance about why he was being questioned. He was a decent actor but, from time to time, his eyes darted nervously to the door as though he hoped someone would come in to rescue him from the ordeal. By the time the interview was winding down, Danny appeared scared. He looked so young, I thought. He should be sitting in a college classroom, and not mixed up with a kidnapping.

Having watched the two brothers, it was difficult for me to work up my anger toward them. The older one came across as mentally disturbed, and the younger man struck me as clueless. Now that they were both in custody, I could almost felt sorry for them. As I did for the murderous Sweeney Todd when—at the end of the play—he becomes undone and begins weeping over the body of his dead wife.

Rodriguez returned to the room with the Lieutenant.

He said, "Mrs. Crane, I want to thank you for coming in to identify these men."

"So what happens to them now?" I asked.

"We'll have to check with the State's Attorney's Office but, from what Detective Rodriguez has told me, I think your identification will be enough to charge them. Of course, then we'll begin a more comprehensive investigation. Thanks to Mrs. Adelle, we already have a good idea as to the location of the cabin where you were being held. She told us her brother and his friends used it as a hideout when they were kids. She's sorry she didn't think of it sooner. Anyway, I suspect we'll find the pontoon boat nearby as well."

"Don't forget about the man who works at Pop's Outfitters. I'm sure he's the one who let them know we were out on the river."

"It's in our notes from your first interview. Don't worry, we'll pursue every lead. So, you're free to go now. We'll be in touch if we need more information from you and, of course, we'll let you know when a trial date is set. Thanks again for coming to our office. I believe you have a friend waiting for you."

Delcie was talking with one of the deputies when I rolled my walker out to the waiting area. She saw me, and ended her conversation.

"They sure have a lot of shit going down in Putnam County," she whispered, as we left the building.

"More than we have in Alachua?" I asked, slipping into the front seat of her car. Delcie folded my walker, stowed in the back, and got in the driver's seat.

"Maybe not. Guess I'm just of out of the loop with my old buddies at ASO. So, did you make the guys?"

"It was a no-brainer," I said. "I felt a bit sorry for them."

"That's too generous, Lor. They might have hurt you a lot worse if you hadn't escaped."

"I guess so, but seeing them in jail they didn't seem threatening. The older brother, you know, he was in the Iraq war. I wonder if that's what caused him to be so violent and depressed?"

"Yeah, could be. There are a lot of stories about emotional problems vets have when they return home. The war seems to do a real number on their heads and bodies. Guess you'll never really know. On a more cheerful subject, do you have time for lunch? We could stop at Leonardo's 706 on the way to your condo."

"It's tempting, but I can't. I have a doctor's appointment at one. I really appreciate you're coming with me this morning."

Delcie dropped me at the condo where I picked up my car, and went on to the doctor's office.

Later, when I arrived at the theater, I was immediately greeted by Jeremy.

"Well, look at you. Is that your new Prada?" he asked, looking at the shoe boot I got at the doctor's.

"Don't make fun, Jeremy. Renee is going to have a fit!"

"Renee will have a fit about what?" she said, joining us in the lobby. She took one look at my foot, and asked, "And how long will you have to wear that godawful bootie?"

"The doctor said it might take about six weeks for the toe to heal. But at least I can use a cane now instead of the walker. And if I rest my foot and use ice packs—when I'm not in rehearsals—it might heal quicker."

"That's just great," she said. She studied my feet for a moment, and added, "I guess we could get your costume lengthened so it would mostly cover the boot."

I looked down at my cane, and gave her a pleading look.

"Oh, all right. Mrs. Lovett can walk with a cane. Don't you think so, Jeremy?"

He nodded. "As long as she doesn't use it on me."

I poked him with my elbow, and said, "Thank you so much, Renee. I promise you, I'll be very focused on my performance. It will be my entire life for the run of the play. No more problems. I promise."

"So, did they catch the men who kidnapped you?" she asked.

"Yes, they're in custody right now."

"Good. Someday you'll have to tell me the real story. Not the version you gave the cast."

Her insightful observation made me smile. "I will," I said.

Renee walked away, and Jeremy and I sat down on one of the benches in the lobby.

"I'd like to hear the real story, too." he said. "Apparently, your visit to the sheriff's office this morning went well. You must be pleased they caught your kidnappers so quickly."

"I am, and I don't want to talk about it anymore. I'm here to work. That's it."

He took my hand, and gave me a searching look. "Did you give any thought to my question last night?"

I thought about it, and said, "You know, Jeremy, I do find you very attractive, but…"

He smiled, moved closer to me, and repeated, "But?"

"But you heard what I told Renee. I really mean it. I can't have anymore distractions while I'm working. It wouldn't be fair."

He put his arm around me. "Don't you think some passion might enhance your performance rather than detract from it? You know, get your emotional juices revved up."

I laughed. He had a point, but I wasn't ready to concede it just yet. I needed recovery time from all that had happened during the past week.

"We'll see," I said, returning his smile.

Chapter 21

Several weeks passed from the time I identified my kidnappers at the sheriff's office. I had just returned from a final costume fitting when Homer called.

"Lorelei, in case you haven't already heard, both Joshua and Danny Tyler are still in jail," he said. "They were denied bond. You know, kidnapping is a life felony in Florida."

"Thanks, Homer, I hadn't heard about it. Frankly, I've been totally wrapped up in rehearsals. What about the guy at the canoe rental place?"

"Oh, the one at the outfitters in Palatka. He's been questioned. It turns out he's a cousin of the brothers. Lonnie Tyler's his name."

"A cousin? How cozy."

"At first he denied any involvement with the brothers. Unfortunately for him, his cell phone records showed him calling Joshua Tyler around the time you left for the river. Oh, and the pontoon boat they used in the kidnapping? It was his boat. Not too smart."

"No kidding?" I said. The guy was real doofus, I thought, just like Jeffrey described him. "I thought he was the one. You know Homer, it didn't occur to me until now, but how did the kidnappers know which one of us to grab?"

He chuckled. "How do you think someone would identify you, Lorelei?" I blushed with embarrassment, and instinctively touched my hair. "Oh," I said. "Of course, the redhead." I thought for a moment, and asked, "Now, I wonder if the cousin was also involved with Kincaid's murder. Jeffrey told me he'd been a regular at the bar for several months."

Homer said, "That may be a leap. Detective Watson told me he sent someone over to Palatka to interview the man. I don't know if they got anything, or not."

"What about the bartender at Charley's? The detective told me he was going to have him interviewed again."

"I honestly don't know. I only get bits and pieces of information when I happen to run into Kyle—Detective Watson."

"Well, I appreciate everything you've told me, Homer. Like I said, I've been out of the loop getting ready to open the play."

"Just as well you left it alone. Say, how about dinner one night this week?" he asked.

"I'd love to, but I promised my director I'd focus all my energy on the play. It's very intense—as you know from having seen the movie."

"All right," he said. "But after the opening, I insist on taking you out for a celebration."

I realized, by having excused myself from any personal relationships with Jeremy and Homer, I had avoided potential emotional distractions. At least until the play opened. I actually enjoyed the intensity of being absorbed by nothing other than my performance, and that of my fellow cast members. It was the life in which I felt the most clarity and vitality.

Earlier in the morning, I watched an interview with Meryl Streep in which she talked about her preparation for a role. She said she had to *wrangle* all of her personal elements together to fit the character. And then, she said, she was simply forced to reassemble herself. Her description was abstract, but very intriguing. I intuitively understood what she meant by it.

I was mentally gathering all of the elements which enabled me to inhabit the character of Mrs. Margery Lovett—sinister schemer, and sometimes charming shopkeeper. According to the Robert Mack anthology, patrons of Mrs. Lovett's were divided among those who thought her incomparably attractive, those who compared her "set smile [to that] of a ballet-dancer, which is about one of the most unmirthful things in existence," and others who said that there was "a lurking devil in her eye." Mack's work contained the original nineteenth-century serial. Reading it inspired me to make use of my cane as a prop to express the dominating aspect of her personality.

I was preparing to go to the gym for a workout, when Jeffrey called.

"I'm back," he said. "Did you miss me?"

"Jeffrey, it's so good to hear from you. Yes, I missed you. So much has happened."

"You can tell me about it over lunch, how about it?"

Another distraction to avoid? Oh, well, I have to eat, and I wanted to tell him everything that had happened in his absence.

"All right, I can be free by one o'clock. Where shall we meet?"

"How about Charley's? I've missed their burgers. They don't quite get the American burger thing in Costa Rica."

I laughed. Always burgers, beer, and babes—or boys. In any case, it would feel good to be back in Jeffrey's simple collegiate world again. "Okay, I'll be there."

I showered and changed at the gym, and made it to Charley's a few minutes before one. The bartender gave me a nod of recognition, and I was tempted to try and talk with him about the Tyler's cousin. Just then, Jeffrey walked in.

He took one look at my cane, and said, "What the hell happened to you? Fall off of the stage?"

"Very funny. I'll tell you all about it later. I need to sit."

We settled ourselves in the booth we always sit in and, after we ordered, we exchanged pleasantries. He told me about his time in Costa Rica, and relayed some humorous anecdotes involving him and his students. Finally, he said, "Enough about me. What's the story with the foot and cane? You said on the phone that a lot happened while I was gone."

"Yes, there's quite an adventure to tell you about."

"I'm eager to hear it. By the way, I talked with Bear, and he told me Becky's not back in town yet."

"No, Becky isn't back," I said. "I think it might be a while before she's well enough to return. I haven't talked with her. Every time I call, her parents say the same thing—she's getting better. That's all."

"Hmm, poor kid. Has anybody found out what happened to her?"

"That's what I wanted to tell you about."

I told him about contacting his friend, Sharon Adelle, and our trip down the Ocklawaha. He was shaken to hear about my kidnapping experience. I told him they wanted the names of all the Earth Save members responsible for blowing the dam, and J.T. actually believed both Jeffrey and I were involved.

Jeffrey was wide-eyed as I recounted the story of my escape from the men, and my subsequent experience identifying the two brothers. I also told him what I had just learned, from Homer, about the complicity their cousin—the same guy who hung out at Charley's.

It took him a few moments to digest it all. Finally, he said, "When you said a lot happened, that was an understatement. My God, Lorelei, you could have been killed—like Stoker. All because some good old boys were out to get revenge for the Rodman."

"Don't forget about the grandfather's and little nephew's near drowning. But you're right. Mostly it was about revenge over the Rodman. Now the problem is that nobody has yet connected my kidnappers to Kincaid's death, or to whatever happened to Becky. I definitely think the two are linked."

"You said the cousin, the same guy who hangs out here, was also involved in the scheme. He's your connection. We probably haven't been as careful as we should have been around here."

Before I could respond, our food arrived, and we ate in silence. I could tell Jeffrey was brooding about the situation. He finished his burger, wiped his mouth with a napkin, and said, "Just a minute, Red, I'm going to talk to the bartender." He picked up his drink, and went over to the bar. I followed him.

After explaining why he hadn't been around for awhile, and having a brief conversation about mutual friends, Jeffrey got to the point. He said, "You know the heavy set guy in the plaid shirt who hangs out here on the nights we have our meetings? You know, he sits on the same stool at the end of the bar—over there. Lonnie's his name."

The bartender gave Jeffrey a thoughtful look before he replied, "Yeah, yeah, I know who you mean. Kind of a country dude."

"That's the one," Jeffrey said.

"What about him?"

171

"When Lorelei and I were in here about a month ago, she told me he was staring at her."

The bartender looked inexplicably relieved by the comment and, giving Lorelei the once over, he said, "Can't blame him for that."

It was intended to be humorous, but we didn't laugh.

Jeffrey said, "Seriously, man, do you know if he ever got into it with Stoker?"

The bartender's friendly smile vanished into a wary frown. The question seemed to put a chill on the conversation. He glanced around to see if anyone was within earshot. Finally, he lowered his voice, and said, "Look, man, I'd like to help you, but the cops have been in here recently asking me about this dude. They told me I shouldn't talk to anybody about him."

Jeffrey leaned in, and put his elbows on the bar. He, too, spoke in a soft voice. "I understand, but you know me—I don't talk to cops. I'm only asking if the two of them, you know, maybe got into some kind of fracas. That kind of thing."

Charley absently picked up a glass to dry with his bar towel. "Okay, but remember I didn't talk to you about this. I'll deny it if you say so. I got a license that's already being looked at. You know how these college kids fake their IDs."

"How long have you known me? I won't say anything," Jeffrey assured him.

"Okay, yeah, they talked, and sometimes it got pretty heated. Both of them could really lay down a lot of booze."

"What'd they talk about?" I asked.

He glanced back at me, standing halfway behind Jeffrey. "Mostly war stuff. The heavy guy was in the first Gulf War. They had that in common, along with both being in special ops—or something like it. They argued a lot over politics."

At that moment a couple of college students sat down near us.

Charley said, "That's all, I can't say no more." He moved down the bar in front of the new customers, and said, "What can I get you guys? You got ID?"

We returned to our booth. I slid in alongside Jeffrey so we could talk quietly. It was my turn to ask the questions.

"Before you left on your trip, I asked you if anyone in Earth Save was responsible for bombing Rodman. You told me you didn't know. Is that still the truth?"

He squirmed a bit, and gave me a hard look before replying. "I told you then I only had a suspicion. Nothing concrete."

"And have you found out your suspicion was correct?" I persisted.

"Look, Bear and Stocker were close. They'd both served in Iraq together. It's possible, if Stoker was involved, Bear would be, too. But we don't really know, do we? The one thing I do know is that Bear is seriously paranoid about being found by whoever killed Stoker. You know he's been hiding out."

"He should be scared. This J.T. Tyler is a psycho," I said. "Fortunately, he and his brother are locked up in jail. Then what about Becky? She and Bear were dating."

Jeffrey simply shrugged, "Don't go too far with this, Lorelei. Bear said nothing more than that he's concerned about her."

"What about Tim Grantly? He's disappeared, as well."

"Look, it's all possible, all right. I don't know, and I really don't want to know."

"Well, it sounds like your doubts confirm what I've suspected right along—one, or more of them may have been involved with whoever blew up the dam."

Suddenly, Jeffrey grabbed my arm. He gave me a fierce look and said, "I hate it that you're still pressuring me with these questions. I know you have a relationship with Detective McBride. I've asked you before to promise you'd never ever discuss our conversation about this. You know what will happen to our friends if anybody even so much as suspects their involvement. They've all been through enough already. You've got to leave it alone. Promise me—on the soul of our dead baby. Promise."

It was the first time, in many years, since Jeffrey had mentioned the miscarriage I suffered in our car accident. I was shocked, and near tears.

"Oh my God, Jeffrey. Yes, I promise," I said, barely able to speak for the upwelling of emotion. I pulled my arm from his grasp.

We stared at each other, and remained in pain filled silence for several moments.

Finally, I contained my emotions, and said, "Don't worry; I won't reveal any of what we've talked about. Anyway, there's a new guy, Detective Watson, who's in charge of the case, and he believed Stoker's death had to do with a drug deal."

Jeffrey momentarily looked away, and wiped tears from his eyes before responding. "I can see how he decided that," he said. "Everybody knew Stoker was dealing, but I always thought he was real careful. I think he did some of it right here at Charley's—I mean outside. He'd stay at the bar until closing. It was like he did it so they'd know where to find him."

I said, "Detective Watson's rethinking the motive since he's learned about my kidnapping. And then there's the kidnappers cousin. It's too much of a coincidence his making friends here with Stoker."

As if he hadn't heard what I said, Jeffrey gave me a soulful look, "Lorelei…"

"Please don't, Jeffrey. Let's not go there. Past is past."

He nodded, and took a sip of his drink. The emotional moment passed.

As if nothing had happened between us, I said, "I'm just glad the police are following up on it. At least, if J.T. and his accomplices had an idea, maybe other than Stoker, who else might have been involved in the bombing, they wouldn't have resorted to kidnapping me."

Jeffrey said, "Except, maybe that's what they wanted to do with Becky."

"You mean kidnap her, like they did to me, to try and find out?"

"It makes sense, doesn't it? If they wore ski masks, and came after her that night it's what may have caused her to run into the creek. That would shock anyone."

"You may be right, Jeffrey. I'd like to know the real story—it might help Becky's recovery."

"Now, Red, please don't tell me you're going to stay in the thick of all this. After what you've already been through?"

I put up my hands in protest. "Oh, no, I've been a diligent little actress. I've been so wrapped up in the theater; you're actually the first non-actor friend I've met in weeks. And, speaking of the theater…"

"I know, you've got to get back. Me, too. We collected so damn much stuff on our field trip, and now it has to be classified and organized. It's going to keep us busy for quite a while."

I promised to let Jeffrey know if I learned anything more as a result of the GPD's new investigation. We parted with an embrace that spoke the unspoken about our forever connection to one another. He had touched me about a time in our lives that I had long since confronted, and I couldn't afford to revisit. As for Jeffrey, his regrets appeared to be coming with age.

I returned home to spend the afternoon listening to the audio tapes I had made during rehearsal. The day passed quickly. I was having a light dinner, before going to the theater, when I got a call from Homer.

"Did you watch the news?"

"No, I didn't. What happened?"

"Joshua Tyler committed suicide."

I gasped. "How could he? Wasn't he in jail?"

"Yes," Homer said. "It happens."

Chapter 22

Renee's intuition was correct. My friend, Cassie Woodruff, stepped into my role on the second night after our opening. Mother had a massive stroke. By the time I reached South Florida, she had died. I was inconsolable at having missed seeing her before, and I felt guilty at not having visited her during the summer, as I had intended to do.

After the cremation, I drove to the old orange grove behind our home. I scattered her ashes among the trees, as she had requested. Though it was late summer, and the oranges had already set, memory filled my nostrils with the familiar sweet scent of orange blossoms. The aroma evoked so many images of my father, and of my childhood, that I was unable to stop the flow of tears—as though I had held them back through all the years since his death.

Mother's friends at the retirement home were very sweet when I met with them during their afternoon bridge game. They told me how proud mother was of me. They said she often talked about how I had fulfilled her dream to be an actress. I took a few of her belongings—a photo album, some jewelry, and her favorite cashmere cardigan. I arranged for the rest of her things to be donated to the women's shelter thrift shop.

I moved through the official arrangements as though in a dream. She had prepared her own obituary for the newspaper, and had done estate planning with her lawyer, the bank, and with her accountant. I called our few remaining relatives to tell them of mother's passing. No one was surprised. It reminded me that when you reach advanced age; death is a predicable event.

After all the details were completed, I turned off my cell phone, and locked myself in my hotel room for two days with the drapes drawn shut, and the TV on mute. I occasionally ordered food from room service, but ate little. I was grieving, and also contemplating what it meant to my life to be without my mother. We had our differences, as they say about most mothers and daughters. Daddy died while I was still a teenager, and mother often told me she had to act the part of both parents. She could be very tough, but I always knew she loved me. Despite the fact that we sold our family's house, when mother moved to the retirement village, it was she who still represented home in my mind. So, I thought, I was now officially without a home, and—despite my middle age—an orphan, but for my memories.

On the third morning, I opened the drapes to blinking bright sunshine. A look in the mirror revealed that my eyes were still swollen from crying. I felt emotionally numbed, and knew it was time to leave. I checked out of the hotel and, as I drove onto the Turnpike, the old Paul Simon lyric came to mind, "nothing but the dead and dying back in my home town."

I called Delcie when I got back to my condo.

"Lorelei, why haven't you returned my calls? When I called the theater looking for you, they told me about you mother. I've been trying to reach you for days. You had your cell phone turned off, didn't you?"

"Sorry, Del. I haven't listened to my messages. There was a lot I had to do, and I just needed some alone time."

"Understood. Are you all right? How about if I come over?"

"No, I'm doing all right. It was just such a shock, you know."

"I can imagine. Did you have a funeral, or what?"

"No, she wanted to be cremated. I scattered her ashes around our old orange grove."

"It must have been tough."

"Oh, yes, it was hard all right. I knew I'd lose her someday, especially after she had the mini-stroke last year."

"But you're never prepared, are you? I just can't imagine what it'll be like when I lose my mama. I'm going to be a basket case. The best thing is for you to get back to work. When are you going to the theater?"

"I don't know. I have to call Renee and see when she wants me."

"Listen, this may not be a good time, but do you want to hear the latest on the Kincaid case?"

"I guess so. I haven't even thought about it."

"I have this friend at the sheriff's department," Delcie said. "We used to work together at ASO when I was a deputy. Anyway, I had asked her to let me know if she heard of any major developments in the case. She called yesterday."

"No kidding. What did she tell you?"

"She said GPD was going to be making an arrest in the Kincaid case within the next day or two."

"Did she say who?"

"No, but she thought it was a Putnam County man."

"Do you think it was J.T.'s brother, Danny?"

"She said someone was to be arrested. Danny's already in jail."

"Then it must be the cousin. I knew it."

"Well, if you want to find out, you'd better call McBride. Or, better still, call Detective Watson since he's handling the case."

"No, I'll call McBride. Watson probably wouldn't tell me anything."

"Well, I thought you'd want to know. Anyway, sweetie, I can't tell you how sorry I am for your loss. No matter how old you are, losin' a mama has got to hurt a lot. You know I'm here for you. Call me anytime."

"Okay, Del. Thank you. I'll let you know if I find out anything from Homer. Take care, and Del…"

"What?"

"Make time to go see your mama."

I knew it would be too late to go to the theater, so I decided to talk to Homer before calling Renee.

"Lorelei? I tried to call you this weekend—remember your promise? After the opening you were going to let me take you to dinner. Didn't you get my messages?"

"I've been down in South Florida since Saturday. My mom died."

"Oh, I'm sorry to hear that. Was it sudden?"

"Yes, a massive stroke. I just got back into town today."

"When I couldn't reach you, I thought…well, forget what I thought. Is it too soon for you to go out? If you're up to it, how about having dinner with me tonight? That is unless you're going to the theater."

"No, it's too late to go to the theater. Besides, I don't think I'm ready to get back into it just yet. But, I would like to have dinner with you."

We agreed to meet at an Italian restaurant downtown.

I called Renee, and told her I was back in town. She expressed her condolences. Next she told me how well Cassie had done in the role of Mrs. Lovett. My ego was bruised, although I guessed she thought it would be reassuring for to me to know that the show went on smoothly during my absence. I was even afraid, in the next sentence, she would say she was replacing me with Cassie.

Instead, she said, "But of course Cassie isn't Lorelei Crane. She has a lot of promise, but she's still so young. When can we expect you to come back, dear?"

"If you don't mind, how about if I return for the Saturday matinee? That will give me a day to refresh myself on my lines, and it'll be a good warm-up for the evening performance."

"Are you sure you're ready?" she asked.

"Yes, Renee. You've been very generous giving me the leave time, but I think the best thing for me will be to get back to work. I'm sure my mother would want it that way."

Homer and I met at the restaurant, and chose to eat out on the patio. Despite the daytime summer humidity, afternoon showers had cooled things off, and even provided a light breeze. My appetite suddenly returned. I felt ravenous when the waiter presented us with the menus, and told us about their specials. I wanted to order everything, and settled on clams and linguine.

Homer watched me, with amusement, as I began devouring the garlic bread, and paused only long enough to take sips of wine.

"I always enjoy taking a woman to dinner who has a hearty appetite," he said.

"Sorry," I replied, feeling embarrassed by the way I was stuffing my mouth. "It's just that I haven't really eaten much for the past week. And I love Italian food."

"I'm glad. You know it's been quite a while since we had a meal together."

"Oh, the pizza fight," I said. "It all seems silly now in the greater scheme of things. Tell me, how is Bobby doing? Are you having a good summer with him?"

"Bobby is doing quite well, thanks for asking. I don't think I told you, but he's just finished the drama camp, at the Hippodrome State Theater, and he loved it. Who would of thought? My son the actor. It was his mother's idea."

"Have you taken him to see our play?"

"No, I wanted to talk with you about it first. I didn't know if it was appropriate for his age. The movie was rated R."

"I think he'd enjoy it. It's not graphically gory like the movie. Why don't you bring him to the matinee this Saturday?"

"Would he get a chance to talk with you? I think he'd be more impressed with an actor than he is with detectives."

"Sure. I'd love to meet him."

Our food came, and I was in heaven. I tried to pace myself, and savor every delicious bite. Candles were lit on the tables, and Homer and I talked as though we were just two ordinary people on a date. I was glad he didn't ask too many questions about my mother, and the trip down south. It made the evening relaxing and enjoyable.

When we had finished our tiramisu and were drinking our second espressos, I decided it was time to inquire about the murder investigation

"I heard there was going to be an arrest in the Kincaid case," I said.

"Who told you that?" he asked, pulling a stern Detective McBride face. "Oh, don't tell me. It was Delcie. She seems to know everything that goes on in our office. What else did she tell you?"

"Nothing really. Just that an arrest was imminent. Can you tell me more about it?"

He pulled a pack of cigarettes out of his jacket, tapped one on the table, and lit up before answering. "Okay, you've certainly paid a heavy price to be involved in this case. I guess you're entitled."

"Thank you."

"After Joshua Tyler's suicide, his brother Danny loosened up a bit. They offered him a lighter sentence in exchange for information about the Alachua County case. They didn't really expect him to take it, since it was his own cousin who was the primary suspect."

"Did he?"

"Yes. Apparently, he had a long standing grudge against the cousin. I don't know the details. You already know, Joshua Tyler was determined to get revenge on the people who breached the dam. He enlisted his n'er-do-well cousin—who regularly went to the VA in Gainesville—to find out where Earth Save held their meetings. That wasn't too difficult since the group is well known among Gainesville environmentalists."

"And that's why he was hanging out at Charley's? He was a spy."

"Yes. According to Danny Tyler, the cousin observed members of Earth Save getting together, in a back booth, before or after the meetings. Adam Kincaid was regularly one of them, and Lonnie Tyler managed to strike up a relationship with him. They were both veterans."

"The bartender at Charley's told you about their relationship."

McBride gave me a quizzical look. "So, you know all this already?"

"Not all of it. Please, go on."

He took a few drags on his cigarette, brushed the smoke away that had drifted toward me, and continued. "Tyler eventually got Kincaid to admit that he had blown up bridges and dams in the military—the bartender overheard the discussion. Kincaid was quite drunk, and hinted he'd done some demolition work here, at home. That was all J.T.'s cousin needed to hear."

"He assumed Kincaid was referring to the Rodman," I said.

"Yes. At that point, he must have decided the people in the back booth were Kincaid's co-conspirators. Eventually, he was able to find out some of their names."

"That's pretty damming evidence, isn't it?"

"Not quite enough. Danny Tyler maintains his brother was innocent of murder, and he never went as far as directly accusing his cousin of it.

"So did they get anything else on him?"

"Detective Watson had Lonnie Tyler's car impounded. They found forensic evidence that places Kincaid in the vehicle. They also have the bartender's testimony that Lonnie was at the bar the night Kincaid was killed. The bartender said Kincaid was too drunk to drive home—he lived nearby—so he left on foot. Lonnie Tyler left the bar shortly afterward. We can fill in the rest."

"Was J.T. Tyler in on the murder?" I asked. "Wouldn't it have taken two men to kill Kincaid, and dump his body into the creek?"

"Not necessarily. If he was as drunk and drugged out as the bartender suggested, it could have been done by one man." McBride shrugged. "I guess we won't know all the details unless Lonnie confesses. Which, by the way, he's likely to do. Watson's got a pretty tight case against him now."

"So it was probably Lonnie and J.T. Tyler who went after Becky," I said. I don't think Danny Tyler would have done it."

"You're probably right. Danny Tyler swears he never did anything more than help his brother kidnap you. He said they were on their way to go fishing when J.T. got a call, from Lonnie, about "the Gainesville redhead" being on the river. J.T. went back to the truck and grabbed some stuff—including the ski masks—and they set off to find you. Danny said it was the first he knew what his brother meant to do. After they had you locked away, they pulled the pontoon boat up and hid it along the shore. By the time they got back to the cabin, you were gone. They started searching for you in the woods, but it got dark, and they gave up. J.T. called Lonnie to come get them."

"I'm lucky it took them so long to hide the boat, or they would have found me."

"I'm told Danny's very remorseful about the incident. You've certainly been through a lot recently between the kidnapping and the death of your mother. How are you holding up?"

"I'm not really sure," I responded, and suddenly felt overcome by a wave of sadness. Though I tried to hold them back, I felt tears leaking from my eyes.

Homer reached across the table, and put his hand on mine. "You're going to be okay. I promise. It'll just take time," he said, in a soft and soothing voice.

I knew he was right, but the compassionate look on his face made the tears flow harder. I stood up, and excused myself as I fled to the privacy of the bathroom.

Chapter 23

"I can't believe it. Are you really planning to leave Gainesville?" Delcie asked, with a look of distress written all over her face. "Forever, or what?"

I had asked both Delcie and Jeffrey to meet me for lunch. I wanted to tell my dearest friends what I intended to do after the play closed. Delcie arrived at the restaurant before Jeffrey. I was glad to have a chance to see her alone.

"Forever? No, at least I don't think so. I just need to get away from Florida for a while. The past few years have been too heavy—you know what I mean. And, I don't feel like I'm growing here anymore, as an actress. I need new experiences and challenges. I've got to nourish myself."

"I understand. Where will you be going?"

"San Francisco. Jeremy's got a part in a play at the American Conservatory Theater, he has a sublet, and..." I heard myself blurting out the information until Delcie put up her hand to stop me.

"Jeremy? Lorelei, I just talked with you last week, and you didn't mention any serious plans with him. In fact, I thought you two were cooling it. When did all this happen?"

I felt a little embarrassed at blindsiding her. "Saturday night. We had a late supper together—it was his birthday—and...well, he spent the night with me."

Delcie's eyes widened, she leaned forward, and slapped my wrist. "Why, aren't you something. So, how was it? I mean are the two of you an item now?"

I felt a slow blush rise up my neck. "An item? I've already told you I find him very attractive, and we obviously have a great deal in common. Yes, there's potential for a relationship. He's easy to be with, and he's mature—he knows what he wants out of life."

Delcie shot a quick glance at the restaurant entrance, and said, "Unlike you know who. By the way, you said you invited both of us to lunch. Where is your ex?"

I looked at Delcie's watch. "He'll be along in a minute. Anyway, about Jeremy. He's really helped me through these past few weeks."

"The bedroom, please," Delcie said with an arch look.

"You are so nosy," I said, and lowered my voice to a whisper. "Okay. I can only speak about our one night together. I found him to be a very sensitive lover, and we laughed a lot."

"Uh huh. Sounds like you've got yourself a winner, girlfriend. I'm happy for you, and I'm going to miss you like hell."

"Oh, me too, Delcie. You're my best friend. I expect you to come out to the coast to visit."

"Not the same, but thanks for the offer. Hey, on second thought, maybe I'll set up a branch office out there. We could work together."

I got into her fantasy. "What kind of work? What would we call ourselves?"

She thought a moment and, with a big grin on her face, said, "I know—"Trackers and Thespians, Inc." Most of what I do is hunt for people and you..."

"Thespians?" I repeated. "It's kind of an old fashioned word. How about "Trackers and Players?" A bit racier, don't you think?

We continued brainstorming and giggling at our ideas, when Jeffrey appeared in the doorway. He waved to me as he walked over to our table.

"What are you two so jolly about?" he asked, and sat down facing me, next to Delcie. "I've been summoned, and I am here. What's happening?"

"This is my farewell lunch with my two best friends," I announced.

Jeffrey gave me and Delcie a puzzled look. "Farewell? Where are you going?"

The waiter appeared and handed us menus.

"I'll tell you in a minute. Let's order first. Lunch is my treat."

We quickly made selections from the menu, and the waiter left with our orders.

"I've just been explaining to Delcie that it's time for me to move on."

"What the hell does that mean?" Jeffrey asked. "This is your home."

"To be honest, Jeffrey, much as there are people here whom I dearly love, this isn't home to me. At least not any more—not since Bill and my mother are gone. I feel limited here. Like I told Delcie, I'm not growing, and being enriched in a way I need to be, as an actor."

"What about your history with the Tuscawilla? And the play?"

"Frankly, *Sweeney Todd* hasn't been the biggest success. Maybe too many people saw the movie, or thought they did. Anyway, Renee hoped we'd run over until Halloween, but now she's planning to close in two weeks."

"I'm surprised. I thought it was great. You were terrific in it," he said.

Delcie added, "Me, too. I almost didn't recognize you as that crazy baker woman."

"Thank you. I loved the role. It gave me a chance to be evil and saucy. A nice change after playing all those sensible and long-suffering women of Chekhov's and Ibsen's. Though, don't get me wrong, I adore Chekhov—his plays always make me feel like eating black bread, and tossing down glasses of vodka."

Delcie rolled her eyes, and gave Jeffrey a look. He said, "So, tell us more about your plans. I'm not at all happy about you leaving, you know."

"I know. As for my plans, I'm moving to San Francisco—there's a lot of theater there, and it's a wonderfully stimulating cultural environment. I'll be on the Pacific Ocean, and the weather...well, you've both been there, you know the attraction."

Jeffrey said, "Yeah, great Chinese food, and all of that. Realistically though, do you have a job? A place to stay? I know you Bill left you in good financial shape, but it's very expensive to live in San Francisco."

Delcie kept looking at me. She had her hand over her mouth in a suppressed giggle. I knew she was waiting for me to tell Jeffrey about

Jeremy. I wasn't going to disappoint her. "Actually, I'm going to live with Jeremy Hastings, my co-star." I waited for Jeffrey's reaction before saying more.

He cocked his head and scowled. "I didn't know you two were having an affair. Guess I must have missed more than I thought while I was in Costa Rica. Why didn't you mention it when we had lunch together?"

"I am not having an affair—Jeremy and I are good friends."

Jeffrey snorted in disbelief.

"All right, if you must know, but there was nothing to tell you at the time we had lunch together. It's all happened very recently."

I caught the look on Delcie's face. She was clearly enjoying the exchange between me and Jeffrey.

The food arrived, and we started to eat. Every so often, Jeffrey looked up from his plate to glare at me like a spoiled child. Delcie was unusually quiet. I sensed the mood at the table had soured.

Finally, she said, "C'mon you two. Let's lighten things up. How about a drink to toast Lorelei's adventure? This one will be my treat." She beckoned the waiter and ordered two small bottles of Marquis de la Tour sparkling wine.

When the wine was delivered and served, Delcie raised her glass in a toast, "To Lorelei." She elbowed Jeffrey, who reluctantly stopped eating, and raised his glass as well. Delcie continued, "May you find all the fulfillment and adventure you seek, and then some. Love you, girl!"

We clinked glasses, and Jeffrey's scowl vanished into a rueful smile. "Sorry to be such a jerk, Red. I just can't imagine not having you around—at least in Florida. Of course, I echo Delcie's wishes for you. I want you to be happy—always have."

I looked at the two of them, as I sipped my wine, and felt a sharp pain in my chest. It was all I could do to hold back tears. I had been so weepy the past few weeks; it didn't take much to start me crying. The thought of leaving the two of them made me suddenly gloomy.

"You know, it isn't easy for me to leave here. In a way, you were right, Jeffrey. This is the only home I've known for many years. Tearing myself away from dear old friends, like the two of you.

Believe me, it hurts a lot. Still, I know it's the right thing for me to do."

They both nodded sympathetically.

"When do you plan to leave?" Delcie asked.

"Probably soon after the show closes. I'm thinking of just leasing my condo. I've talked to a realtor about it. I'll put some things in storage, and I'm going to take very little with me. It's going to be a new start."

"What about your car? Will you be driving out? I could go with you," Jeffrey said. "I've got some time coming, and I'd love to go to San Francisco anyway."

I considered the eager look on his face, and had a naughty thought about his real motivation, but I said, "Oh, no, thanks so much. I'm going to sell my car and fly out. I won't need one out there."

He gave a brief sigh of disappointment, and replied, "You given me quite a shock. I thought you wanted us here about the Kincaid case, or to tell us you'd talked to Becky."

I was glad for a change of subject, and said, "Actually, I do have news. Did you know they arrested Lonnie Tyler, and have charged him with Stoker's murder?"

Delcie nodded, and Jeffrey said, "Yeah, I heard about it."

He gave me a cautious look, and added, "In fact, our friends, Bear and Tim have come back to Gainesville."

"That's good. I'm glad for them," I said, and returned his look with a reassuring nod. I knew he was testing whether I would honor the terrible oath of secrecy he made me take.

Delcie said, "So have either of you talked with Becky?"

Jeffrey shook his head.

I said, "No, but I'm going to call her before I leave, and press her parents to let me talk to her. I think she needs to hear what we think happened to her."

"I agree," Delcie said.

Jeffrey looked at his watch.

"I know, you need to get back to the lab. Don't worry, we'll talk before I leave town."

"I love you, you know," he said, getting up from the table. He came over, kissed the top of my head, and whispered, "Always have; always will. If it's going to make you happy, then I'm glad for you." He turned and left.

Delcie took a sip of wine, and said, "I believe him. Jeffrey will always be in love with you. Poor guy, he lost the best. Anyway, I've got to leave, as well. You will not—hear me on this—you will not leave town with just a phone call. I plan to come up, and help you pack your stuff. Remember, I helped you unpack, so it's only proper that I help you to conclude."

"I'll remember, Del. I'd love to have you with me."

"Anyway, I need the closure. It'll be fun—sort of. Just let me know when you're ready."

We stood up and hugged. When we released each other, we both had tears in our eyes.

She said, "Now let's pay the damn bill and get out of here, or I'm going to have a meltdown."

Chapter 24

Once I arrived at the theater, I kept to myself and studied my lines. Despite the passion which had been sparked on the night of his birthday, Jeremy and I agreed we wouldn't sleep together again until the show closed. When we weren't working, there was too much to do before leaving Gainesville, and we both needed our rest to maintain the focus for our performances. It took a lot of restraint, but we were actors, after all. We believed we could continue to play our role as friendly costars, though I sensed other cast members perceived the subtle difference in our relationship.

The next morning, after my lunch with Jeffrey and Delcie, I called Homer. I told him I wanted to talk with him, just not on the phone. He suggested dinner, but I had no time for another leisurely evening with Homer.

"How about lunch?" he asked. "I'll be at the courthouse, and I can pick up some burgers, or fried chicken, and bring them up to your place."

Considering what I was going to tell him, a brief lunch made sense. I agreed, "Lunch is a good idea, but please don't bring burgers. I've been off of meat ever since I read about Mrs. Lovett's pies. How about stopping at Books and Café on NW 13th and 7th Avenue? I love their chimichuri sandwich, and the vegan chocolate cake is to die for."

"Is it all vegan stuff?" he asked. I could hear distaste in his tone.

"Oh, don't worry, you'll find something to eat. I'd really appreciate it, Homer."

"Okay, I'll be up at your place around one, if that's all right."

"Fine. See you then."

I hung up, and was amused imagining Homer McBride, my burly detective friend, going into Books, Inc to pick up our lunch. I wondered if he'd ever even bought a book. Oddly, we had never

190

discussed things like that. I would have to ask him about it. In the meantime, I enjoyed the prospect of finding out what he would choose from the vegetarian menu at the cafe.

Homer showed up a little after one with a bag of food. I took it into the kitchen, and started to set up our plates.

"I see your foot is better. Got the bandages off," he said, standing at the entrance to the small kitchen.

"Yes, I saw the doctor this week. It's a relief that I no longer have to use the cane, although I had built it into my character. What do you want to drink with lunch? Lasagna isn't it? So, you did find something familiar to eat there."

"Yes, but it wasn't easy. I'll just have water."

I set us up at the coffee table in the living room; we sat down on the couch and began eating.

"It's an interesting place, isn't it?" I said.

He nodded, and with a mouthful of food, said, "This lasagna's not bad, but I'm not exactly going to be a regular there."

We continued eating and when he was finished, Homer said, "I did pick up a couple of books while I was waiting for our food."

"Really? What'd you get? We've never discussed our reading tastes."

"Oh, I got a biography of Thomas Jefferson, and Michael Gannon's *Short History of Florida.*"

"So you're a history buff? No mysteries or crime fiction?"

"You're kidding, of course. Why would I read about stuff I live every day? Besides, most of it is…"

"Fiction," I added.

"Not exactly my response, but you're correct."

"I enjoy a good mystery novel, from time to time. It's a great escape."

He said, "I guess it would be if it's not your work. Most of them don't describe how boring our typical day is. I guess that's where the creative writing part comes in. Oh, before I forget, I want to thank you for seeing Bobby when we came to the matinee. We both enjoyed the show. It was the first professional production he's ever seen, and you're the first real actor he's met. He couldn't stop talking about it."

"How sweet. I'm just sorry we didn't get to spend more time together. Things are pretty hectic when we do two shows a day. He seems like a nice young man."

"Thanks, we're working on him. Now, what was it you couldn't talk to be about on the phone?" He pushed his plate aside, and picked up the one with his share of the chocolate cake.

"The play is going to close in two weeks, and I wanted to tell you that I'll be leaving town."

"You have a job in another play somewhere?"

"No, I don't, but I feel I need a major change in my life. You know, as an actor, I've got to fill the well so to speak—have experiences I can draw upon for different roles."

"Where will you be going?"

I told him about Jeremy's invitation to live with him in San Francisco. The non-committal expression on Homer's face didn't change as I described what I hoped to find both in my relationship, and on the West coast.

"You haven't said anything, Homer. What do you think?"

He set his plate down, and moved close to me. "Truthfully, Lorelei? I think you're running away, and it makes me regret…" He didn't end the thought.

"Regret?" I asked, searching his face.

"Yes, regret." He reached over and put his arms around me. There was a tender look in his eyes I'd never seen before. "We've been too long at this," he said, and kissed me—first gently then with more intensity. I yielded to him, but didn't reciprocate his ardor. I felt more comfort in his embrace than sensuality. It was the moment I had sometimes wished for, but it didn't move me.

Finally, he released me, and we simply looked at one another for a few moments before speaking.

"Oh, Homer. I'm really so grateful to have gotten to know you over these past few years. However, you're wrong about my motive in leaving. I'm not running away; I'm running toward a richer future and, with Jeremy, the possibility of the kind of relationship I always hoped for."

Homer drew back, and ran a hand through his hair. He had a defeated look on his face. "I know it's too late for us. My life...well, it's not easy to have any kind of a relationship. My ex-will vouch for that."

I said, "Cheer up; at least, you won't have to worry anymore about my getting into your business."

He smiled. "I guess that's something. But, you have to promise not to get involved in any police work in San Francisco. That's the big time out there. They'd eat you alive."

"I promise," I said, standing up.

He also stood, did a tension relieving neck roll, and bent to collect the plates from the table.

"Just leave them. I've got an early makeup call, and I need to get ready to go to the theater. I'm glad you were able to come over. I want you to come to the cast party the last night of the show. It'll be two weeks from Saturday, at ten."

"I'll try to make it."

"Good, I'll expect to see you there. Now you do know, if ever you're in San Francisco..." I said, putting my arm through his as we started toward the door.

"Right. I'll look you up. Okay, then," he said, and stopped to put his arms around me again. "Even though we didn't see one another all that often, I will miss you, Lorelei Crane. You're a remarkable woman."

It was a brief parting, and I showed him out the door. After he left, I plunked myself down on the couch. I reflected on our meeting with wonderment. Homer McBride, making a play for me at the eleventh hour—no, at the twelfth hour. It was unbelievable. And who would have expected those hugs from the usually cool detective?

I took a deep breath, and decided to finish knitting together the threads of my Gainesville life by calling Becky.

Her mother answered my call.

"Hi, it's Lorelei Crane again. I'd really like to talk with Becky."

"Hello, Lorelei. It's kind of you to call. I'm not sure Becky is ready for her Florida friends yet."

Not ready for her friends? I thought, what does that mean? "Mrs. Haimovitz, I know you're only trying to protect Becky, but I have news that might help her recovery."

"You do? Well, you can tell me, and I'll pass it along to her."

"No, really, I think it best if I talk to Becky directly. Will you at least ask if she wants to talk to me?"

There was a pause during which I heard Becky's voice, in the background, asking who was on the phone. Then the voices were muffled, presumably by her mother covering the receiver with her hand.

"Lorelei? Is that you?" Becky said.

"Becky, I'm so glad to hear your voice. You have no idea how concerned all of us have been about you."

"I know, Mom told me you've called a few times. I just wasn't able...you know."

"It's all right. How are you doing?"

"Well, I still have nightmares occasionally, and I don't like to go out alone. But my memory is beginning to come back. That's a good thing."

"Yes, it is. Do you have any recollection of what happened to you here?"

"It's pretty shadowy," she said. "I remember being with a woman and a dog, in a tent, but I'm not sure how I got there. Do you know?"

I decided it was better not to tell her everything at one time, but I did want to answer her question.

"When you didn't show up at the Earth Save meeting, Jeffrey and Bear..."

"Bear? How is he? I bet he's been worried about me."

"He's fine. Yes, he's been worried like the rest of us. Anyway, that night we all went looking for you. First we went to your cottage. We were kind of spooked by the fact that the lock on the back door was broken. Then, the next day, my friend Delcie and I..."

"Oh, I remember your friend Delcie. She's a private detective."

"Yes. Anyway, we finally found out you were minding a friend's cats, and we went to her house. We found your car, with the door wide open, and the contents of your handbag spilled all over. I'll tell you, we were so frightened for you."

I heard an intake of breath before she said, "You found my car?" In the one short phrase, I heard a combination of fear and recognition.

"Becky, are you sure you want to hear the rest?"

"Yes, I do, Lor. I've had these nightmares, you know? I thought it was just my imagination, but maybe it was real. I need to know."

"Okay. So, when we found the scene outside Candace's house, we suspected someone had scared you so badly that you ran into the creek. First we broke into the house, and looked for you. Then, because it was raining, and too dark for us to look in the creek, we called the police. By the time they searched they didn't find any trace of you."

I could hear her breathing more rapidly, but she didn't say anything.

"Becky, I don't think you should listen to any more of this." The voice was her mother's. I guessed she had picked up an extension.

"Please, Mom, I do need to hear it. Will you please get off the line and let Lorelei continue?"

There was a click as her mother apparently complied with Becky's request.

"What happened after that?" Becky asked.

"The next we heard you were spotted, by your friend, at the farmer's market with some homeless woman. Your friend called the police. Your parents, who had come to Gainesville to look for you, took you home the next morning."

There was a long pause again.

"Some of it has been coming back to me, like in a dream," Becky said. "There are these two men in ski masks that pulled up behind me as I was getting out of my car at Candace's house. They came toward me with guns, and I was afraid they were going to kill me, like they did Stoker. I threw away my handbag, thinking I'd distract them, and I raced down into the creek—to get away. I remember it was raining, and the water started rushing against me. I couldn't move fast enough in the sandy bottom. You know, it was like in a nightmare where everything is in slow motion. I kept tripping, and grabbing at branches along the bank. I stumbled through the creek for what seemed like a long time. I kept on going because I was afraid they were following me. I hoped they'd give up when it got dark enough. Then, I remember falling and hitting something hard. The next thing I knew I heard a dog barking. He was on the bank above me, and it was daylight. Lorelei, it was all so terrifying. It can't be real, can it?"

"I'm sure it was real. It fits with what we know."

"Really? So, it wasn't just my imagination. Who were the men? Have they been caught?"

"Yes, one of them committed suicide—in jail. Another man has been arrested and charged with Stoker's murder. We have good reason to believe they are the same two men who were stalking you that day."

"Oh, Lorelei, I can't tell you how important it is for me to know that. I thought a lot of what I remembered was just all in my head. So, they've been caught. But why? Why did they do it?" she asked.

"Revenge. They thought Stoker was the one who blew up Rodman Dam, and they were trying to find out who else was in on it."

"Oh," she said, "Lorelei, that's just what I was afraid of from the moment I heard about Stoker—that whoever killed him would be after some of us, too."

"I can understand why you were so afraid. Anyway, dear, it's all over now. I'm glad you're beginning to recover."

"Yes, the doctor thinks I'm making good progress. Lorelei, will you do me a favor?"

"What is it?"

"Will you let Bear know I'm going to be all right? His cell phone doesn't seem to be working. Maybe he could call me."

"Sure. You just keep on taking good care of yourself. I'm going out to San Francisco in a couple of weeks. I'd love to have you visit me out there—when you're ready to take a trip." And then, I thought, I'll tell you about what happened to me on the Ocklawaha.

"Maybe I could do it in another month or so. I love San Francisco," she said.

"I'll send you a card with my address when I get out there. In the meantime, be well. There are lots of people in Gainesville who care about you. Can I tell Jeffrey it's okay to call you?"

"Jeffrey? Yes, I'd love to hear from him."

"Okay, then."

"Thank you so much for calling, Lorelei. You really have cleared up a lot for me. I can't wait to tell my folks and the therapist everything you've told me."

I flipped my cell phone shut, stood up, and stretched. I knew I would have to call everybody to tell them about my conversation with Becky, and what really happened to her at Candace's house that evening. I still didn't know who, if anyone, in Earth Save had been responsible for breaching Rodman Dam. In my heart, I no longer suspected Becky was involved, though she might have known who was. In any event, with Kincaid's murderers brought to justice, my promise to her and to Jeffrey had been more than fulfilled.

I looked out the window at the flashes of sunlight on Lake Alice. I'll miss this view, I thought. But every time I imagined living in San Francisco, I'd get shivers of excitement.

I picked up my notebook from the table, and re-read my notes from the Meryl Streep interview I had seen. During the interview she described the uncertainty of an actor's life. It is true, in our profession, unemployment is a common experience between jobs. We tolerate the uncertainty because the reward is the wonderful intensity we experience when we are working. Yet, when it's over, we have to come back to earth and live in the real world until the next role. She believed this was what caused actors to live in the moment—the only real way to live.

Yes, I thought, I'm going to try to live a more authentic and present oriented life. I thought of Jeremy, and called him. I felt a tingle of pleasure when I heard his voice.

The party began as soon as the set was struck, after the last performance. Jeffrey, Delcie, and even Homer came. I had invited

Sharon Adelle, and the two hunters who rescued me, Stan and Jake, but they declined the invitation. At least, I had the chance to thank them again for their kindness. As I surveyed the room—the sights and sounds of the festivities—I thought about my mother. How much she would have enjoyed attending my performance, and this event. If only she had lived long enough.

The party would be my farewell meeting with fellow cast members and friends. I was talking with Cassie Woodruff, and telling her about my excitement moving to San Francisco, when I spied Jeffrey and Jeremy, across the lobby, at the wine bar. They were having an animated conversation, and suddenly burst into laughter at something one of them must have said. I was glad they were getting along so well.

Cassie drifted away to talk with other cast members, and I remained watching the two significant men in my life. I realized, from a distance, they didn't appear so very different from one another. Jeremy carried himself with a bit more grace, but they both were about the same height and build, and had dark good looks. Yet, how well I knew the differences between them. Jeffrey had said he would always love me, and—to be honest with myself—I felt the same way about him.

I spotted Delcie and Homer sitting on a bench across the lobby. They were talking with Renee. Delcie looked at me, from time to time, as though to say, *are you certain you want to leave all of this*?

Final cast parties are usually emotional events. My fellow actors had become family, for a time, and it was hard to part with them. Yet, as I thought about the life I was about to begin, I had no doubts that it was my time to move on.

A Note About Hogtown Creek

If you want to know about Hogtown Creek, Chris Bird suggests you "put on a pair of old shoes and walk in the creek for a mile or so." He might also have added, "and when you get home, be sure to wash your feet really well since the creek contains a high bacterial count."

Many Gainesville residents are only aware of the creek by the green street signs that mark their crossing. Others know just a small portion of the sandy stream as it meanders through backyards and behind commercial areas. Its shaded canopy varies in density; the banks may be high, eroded, and vegetated with exotics and natives. The adventure of walking the creek is enhanced by discovering ray and sharks teeth, fish spines, and other fossils in its sandy bottom.

Chris Bird heads the Alachua County Environmental Protection Department (EPA) which is a source of technical information and protection of Gainesville Creeks. Here are a few interesting facts to accompany the map included in the front of this book. Hogtown Creek drains most of Northwest Gainesville and has numerous tributaries—the largest being Possum Creek. The Hogtown Creek Watershed encompasses approximately 20 square miles of urban and suburban Gainesville. The stream length, including all mapped tributaries, is 38.5 square miles. The main channel is 11 miles long as it tumbles down about 120 feet from the headwaters to Haile Sink where it recharges the Floridian aquifer which provides our drinking water.

The creek serves as a wildlife corridor for such creatures as raccoons, many species of birds—including songbirds, wading birds, and birds of prey—rodents, armadillos squirrels, opossums, deer, and even coyotes who are known to use the creek corridor at night to hunt.

There is a myth to the effect that Gainesville was once called Hogtown. In fact, Hogtown was an Indian village, near what is currently Westside Park at the corner of 8th Avenue and 34th Street, and one of the earliest settlements in Alachua County. It is believed to have taken its name from the Indian Chief, Hogmaster, who raised and slaughtered hogs. The village is mentioned in Spanish documents as early as the late eighteenth-century. In the 1820s it became a white settlement when the Seminoles were removed by the Treaty of Moultrie Creek. The City of Gainesville was founded in 1854 on a nearby site. An historical marker can be seen outside the Westside Park Recreation Center.

Hogtown Creek and its tributaries have suffered greatly from urban development encroaching on the floodplain, leaky sewers and septic tanks, runoff from residential and commercial properties, flooding which increases erosion and over sedimentation, and animal wastes. There are also sources of chemical pollution from locations such as Cabot Koppers Superfund site and the Gainesville Mall.

The Hogtown Creek, in addition to being an aesthetic ecological feature of Gainesville, has great significance in recharging the aquifer for our drinking water. It is an intact riparian buffer to microorganisms—which are the base of our food chain. Although much of the creek is degraded it has good flow—an average of over nine million gallons a day.

We are fortunate to have a local environmental agency, Alachua County Environmental Protection Department, which monitors the creek and advocates its restoration needs. But preservation can be aided by citizen awareness of their personal impact on this beautiful and valuable ecological site in the middle of Gainesville. That is my hope by featuring it in this book.

A Note About The Ocklawaha River and Dam

For those concerned about Florida's water supply, Cynthia Barnett's (2008) book, *Mirage: Florida and the Vanishing Water of the Eastern U.S.*, is required reading. Barnett points out that after the dam on Florida's Kissimmee River was blown up, it was only a few years before fish, wildlife habitat, and wetlands vegetation reappeared. The same kind of restoration could be expected when the Ocklawaha dam is removed. The reader is urged to go to www.ditchofdreams.com for a look at a newly published history of the Cross Florida Barge Canal.

The Ocklawaha River, the largest tributary of the St. Johns, is one the primary rivers in the state of Florida. It originates from the waters of the Green Swamp—second only to the Florida Everglades in terms of hydrologic and environmental significance to the state—and various lakes in central Florida. It travels for about 80 miles along the western and northern boundary of the Ocala National Forest before merging with the St. Johns River [only 8 miles from the Rodman Dam].The river itself is contained within Marion County, Putnam County, and partially in Lake County while its drainage basin strays into Alachua County, and Orange County (1000 Friends of Florida, Putnam County Environmental Council, and Nelsons Outdoor Resort.com).

Restoration of the Ocklawaha remains a contentious political issue. Gainesville based Florida Defenders of the Environment cited the top ten reasons for restoring the river:

1. Rodman Reservoir is an unhealthy ecosystem. The shallow weed-choked reservoir has experienced poor water quality, resulting in massive fish kills.

2. Greater economic development through increased ecotourism and recreation will result from restoring the Ocklawaha River and its associated 20 natural springs, now submerged. Plus, fishing will continue on the restored river and area lakes.

3. Taxpayer money ($300,000-$500,000 a year) is spent to maintain a dam that serves no purpose. More than seven millions of dollars will soon be needed to repair the dam and lock structures. Restoration of the river will cost $13.9 million.

4. More and better quality water will be available from a restored Ocklawaha.

5. Seventy five hundred acres of forested wetlands will be created by restoring 16 miles of river. Wetlands are one of the most threatened ecosystems in Florida.

6. Endangered species will benefit from breaching Rodman Dam: manatee, black bear, indigo snake and Atlantic sturgeon. DEP studies show the dam is degrading the St. Johns River by blocking natural water and nutrient flows and the movement of animals.

7. Greater fish diversity will return. At least 13 species, eliminated or drastically reduced in the watershed—like the migratory manatee, shad, striped bass, eel—will be allowed to commute freely after the dam is breached.

8. A great number of sport fish, especially largemouth bass which have declined in the reservoir, will return to the river.

9. Federal legal mandates conflict with maintaining the dam on federal land. In 2003, Florida Attorney General Charlie Crist cited the need to avoid this legal conflict and advised Governor Jeb Bush to veto a bill designed to preserve the reservoir. Bush maintained his strong support for restoration in his veto of the bill.

10. It's the right thing to do. The greatest economic and ecological benefits for the state of Florida and its citizens will result from restoring the Ocklawaha River.

For more information, and to learn how you can support restoration of one of Florida's most beautiful rivers go to Florida Defenders of the Environment (www.fladefenders.org), and to the Putnam County Environmental Council (www.pcecweb.org) which is leading a vigorous fight to protect the St. Johns and the Ocklawaha rivers.

Also by M.D. Abrams

Murder at Wakulla Springs: A North Florida Mystery
(Winner of the Florida Book Award for Popular Fiction)

What if an actress, appearing in an Ibsen play, eerily finds herself caught up in a real life drama which mirrors the play, but involves murders and a threat to her own life? Set in the small Florida coastal town of Apalachicola and at Wakulla Springs reputed to be one of the greatest caves on the planet.

Murder on the Prairie: A North Florida Mystery

The threat of development on North Florida's historic and ecologically unique Paynes Prairie State Park Preserve ignites passions, scandal, and murder.

These novels can be ordered directly from the publisher, BookLocker.com, or from your favorite online or neighborhood bookstore.